KAREN BOOTH

—

HIGH SOCIETY SECRETS

HARLEQUIN
DESIRE

Recycling programs
for this product may
not exist in your area.

ISBN-13: 978-1-335-20940-5

High Society Secrets

Copyright © 2020 by Karen Booth

This edition published by arrangement with Harlequin Books S.A.

For questions and comments about the quality of this book,
please contact us at CustomerService@Harlequin.com.

Harlequin Enterprises ULC
22 Adelaide St. West, 40th Floor
Toronto, Ontario M5H 4E3, Canada
www.Harlequin.com

Printed in U.S.A.

Karen Booth is a Midwestern girl transplanted in the South, raised on '80s music and repeated readings of *Forever* by Judy Blume. When she takes a break from the art of romance, she's listening to music with her college-aged kids or sweet-talking her husband into making her a cocktail. Learn more about Karen at karenbooth.net.

Books by Karen Booth

Harlequin Desire

The Eden Empire

A Christmas Temptation
A Cinderella Seduction
A Bet with Benefits
A Christmas Rendezvous

Dynasties: Seven Sins

Forbidden Lust

The Sterling Wives

Once Forbidden, Twice Tempted
High Society Secrets

Visit her Author Profile page at Harlequin.com, or karenbooth.net, for more titles.

You can also find Karen Booth on Facebook, along with other Harlequin Desire authors, at Facebook.com/harlequindesireauthors!

This book is for all women who make a point
of supporting and lifting up other women.
You make the world a better place.

One

Clay Morgan was too much—a skyscraper of a man with stormy blue-gray eyes and a mop of nearly black hair that begged for Astrid Sterling's touch. She watched him from across the room at the bustling cocktail party as he stood apart from the crowd, observing. Taking it all in. An architect, he possessed a brilliant mind, a brain that could create something out of nothing. It was a marvel to see in action, a luxury Astrid had every workday. But Clay also had a stern heart, possibly chiseled out of ice. Or at least that was all Astrid could surmise, judging by the disposition he saved for her.

She'd done nothing to deserve it. Not a thing. And it was slowly driving her mad.

Grant Singleton was hosting this evening, at his showpiece of a home in La Jolla, California. Grant was CEO of the company Astrid worked for, Sterling Enterprises, a real estate development firm started by Astrid's now-deceased ex-husband. Astrid also owned seventeen percent of the company, so she wasn't your average employee. Although Clay, who worked with her on the Seaport Promenade team, treated her as though she was.

She plucked a glass of champagne from a tray when one of the party's servers offered. "Thank you," she said to the young man.

"Beautiful night," he answered, by way of small talk.

Astrid looked over her shoulder. Outside the wall of windows rimming Grant's modern home, tall palms bent in the swift ocean breeze. The fronds chaotically ruffled in the wind, set against an inky, moonlit sky. The scene was like Clay—shadowy and mysterious—but calling to her all the same. She wished she could be out there with him right now, so they could be alone, away from the office, and she could try to shake free some of what was pent up in his head. She was desperate for answers. Why was he so cold and closed off? Why did he treat her with such utter disdain?

"Absolutely gorgeous." The server's voice got her attention.

Astrid turned back, catching him as he stole an eyeful of her. She smiled and ignored the way it made her feel like an object. She was more than used to it by now, and had learned not to acknowledge it or question it or even care. It happened dozens of times a day. Funnily enough, when she'd been a gangly and awkward teen, she would have done anything for that sort of male attention. When she finally grew into her frame and her sharp edges began to round out, her whole world changed—a modeling career, a one-way ticket out of her home country of Norway, and ultimately, a boulder of a diamond from Johnathon Sterling. The marriage didn't last, but she'd had a few years of his love. She was grateful for what it had given her. She certainly wouldn't be standing in this room right now if it hadn't been for him.

"Thank you again," she said to the server, impatient to return her focus to Clay. This was one of the rare times she got to see him away from work, and she wanted to study his interactions with others, particularly his sister, Miranda, who had just arrived. Astrid's connection to Miranda was improbable—Miranda had been married to Astrid's ex-husband, Johnathon, when he died two months ago. Astrid also, quite unfortunately, had learned a terrible secret about the start of Miranda's marriage to Johnathon. Astrid was desperate to keep it buried forever, but it was eating at her nonetheless. Astrid liked Miranda quite a bit. Plus, she knew what it was like to have once been wed to a man who took whatever he wanted.

"Let me know if you need anything," the server said before departing.

What I really need is a map of Clay Morgan, or at the very least, a set of instructions.

On the other side of the room, Grant gently tapped a spoon against his champagne glass, begging for everyone's attention. Tara, the first of Johnathon Sterling's wives, joined him. Together, Tara, Miranda, and Astrid had controlling interest of Sterling Enterprises. The announcement Grant was about to make likely impacted them all, greatly.

"I first want to thank you all for coming this evening. I have several exciting announcements to make." Grant's warm brown eyes lit up with anticipation. He loved his job and was an able company leader.

Clay, for his part, stuffed his hands into his pants pockets and leaned against a nearby column. Astrid couldn't help but admire the long plane of his body—the defined chest currently wrapped up in a well-made black dress shirt, the dip of his trim waist, and the legs that seemed to stretch on for eternity. She marveled at his ability to convey power and brilliance in the most casual of ways, all while he remained oblivious to the effect he had on her and quite possibly, other women.

"As many of you know," Grant continued, "About two weeks ago, on September 7, Sterling Enterprises passed the first round for the Seaport Promenade project with the city. We couldn't have done it without the dedication of the entire team, including Clay Morgan, Astrid Sterling, and of course, Tara." Grant reached for Tara's hand, and Astrid saw the moment when their fingers hooked and their connection became palpable. They'd fallen in love, despite the fact that Tara had sworn there was nothing going on between them. "Which leads me to my next announcement. Tara and I are not only planning to operate the company as co-CEOs from this day forward, we're engaged to be married."

There was a gasp from the throng of guests, followed quickly by a roar of applause and guests hurrying to offer their congratulations. Astrid hung back, and she couldn't ignore the fact that Clay was doing the same. Astrid had her own reasons for being reticent about the purported happy news. She, Tara, and Miranda had a deal. They were supposed to be a coalition within Sterling, and the whole thing had been Tara's idea, a plan hatched after Johnathon divided his majority interest in the company between his three wives. Tara's engagement to the current CEO would at best divide her loyalties, and at worst, tear them away for Miranda and Astrid.

Astrid wound her way through the crowd until she reached Miranda, who was standing not far from Tara and Grant, apparently waiting for the moment when she could congratulate them.

"Did you know about this?" Astrid asked.

Miranda shook her head. "I had my suspicions. It makes perfect sense, doesn't it? They've known each other for years, and the few times I've been around them both, I definitely sensed a spark."

"But co-CEOs?" Astrid asked the question as quietly as possible. "Between that and the engagement, it seems that Tara has fully aligned herself with Grant, when she was supposed to be doing that with us."

Miranda nodded, focusing on Astrid. She was one of the few people who took Astrid seriously. "Let's talk to her, then. See where we stand."

They approached Tara, who seemed totally swept up by the moment. "Can we talk with you?" Astrid was already leading them into a corner of the room for privacy.

"Yes. Of course. What's up?" Tara asked.

"First off, congratulations," Miranda said.

Astrid was more than a little annoyed that she had to be the one solely focused on business right now. "Yes, congratulations. I'm very happy for you both." She scanned Tara's face, which was relaxed and confident. "But I also have a question."

"Let me guess," Tara said. "You're concerned that I'm in too deep with Grant."

"You're getting married and you're co-CEOs. I don't think it's possible for you to be in any deeper," Astrid answered.

"Don't you have to consult with us before you assume the position of co-CEO?" Miranda asked.

"Technically, yes. And of course, you two are able to register your objections, if you have any. But this is good for the three of us. I'm no longer merely floating around the company with an ambiguous role. I have the title and all of the power that affords me. That's good for us. If anything, it protects our interest in the company."

Astrid wished she could be so sure. "As long as you're still dedicated to the Seaport Promenade project." As far as Astrid was concerned, this was the perfect time for her to be selfish and push her own agenda. That project, a large undertaking for the city that involved what would eventually be a vast public space, kept her working with Clay. She very much wanted the chance. If he truly didn't like her, she at least had to figure out why.

"Yes. I need some assurances that it will happen," Miranda added. She had her own reasons for caring deeply about the Seaport. It had been Johnathon's pet project before his untimely death more than two months ago. "Any progress on naming the park after Johnathon?"

"I'm still working on that," Tara said.

Just then, Grant waved Tara over. Clay had joined him, and the two were quickly deep in discussion.

"I hope you can excuse me for one minute," Tara said, not waiting for an answer and marching over to the two men.

"What are those three talking about?" Astrid asked.

"I have a feeling I know," Miranda said. "I think there's big news for my brother."

"One last announcement, everyone," Grant called out before Astrid had a chance to inquire more. "I want to congratulate the firm's star architect, Clay Morgan, on being a finalist for the state Architect of the Year."

Miranda began to furiously clap, and so did Astrid, but her heart was also breaking a little as she watched Clay's reaction. He offered the obligatory smile, but it was so glaringly obvious, at least to her, that he was not enjoying this moment in the spotlight. How sad was that? This was a big accomplishment. What was it about him that he seemed to take no joy in anything?

Astrid felt an urgent need to at least fix that look on his face, and she rushed over to him in Miranda's wake. She watched as Miranda and Clay embraced. There was an obvious warmth between them as brother and sister, a bond that seemed strong and loving. So he wasn't made of pure ice, or at least not when it came to family. Miranda stepped back and Clay's sights flew to Astrid. For a moment, it felt as though her heart was being squeezed like a stress ball as their gazes connected and she tried to decipher what must be going through his head. In that split-second, she reached no conclusion, other than that she wanted to hug him, too, but she was certain he would recoil.

Instead, she did the only thing she could think to do. She offered a handshake. "Congratulations, Clay. It's so exciting. I'm honored to be working with you on the Seaport project. I can't wait for us to start on the next phase together."

Clay looked down at her hand. "Thanks. But I'm going to ask to be taken off the project."

Astrid's heart dropped so low it was currently residing near her feet. "But why?"

"I'm not sure you and I work well together."

It hurt like hell to say that to Astrid, and the devastated look on her stunning face was making it that much more difficult. But it was the truth. They *didn't* work together well. He was endlessly distracted by her. He made mistakes when they worked together and he prided himself on not doing that. He'd made a gaffe on the Seaport Promenade several weeks ago and it could have cost them the entire project. Luckily, Tara had discovered his mistake before the first presentation. The Architect of the Year definitely did not suffer such lapses, and he wanted that award more than anything. Aside from his young daughter and his sister, Miranda, Clay had nothing else in the world to pin any happiness to. His job was a crucial part of his life. It helped to define him.

Astrid—with her willowy legs, sweet personality, and beguiling honey-gold hair—was standing between him and the very function of his brain. They'd been working together for well over a month and things weren't getting better. In fact, they might be getting worse. When she was around, he was all thumbs. He found himself searching for words, and he was a man with a large vocabulary—surely there had to be some verbiage that was easily accessible. But no. Not when Astrid was close.

He instead found himself concentrating on the curve of her full lips, enchanted by her wide cocoa-brown eyes. He couldn't afford to fall for another beautiful face. It had ruined his entire life the other time he'd shown such weakness, for the woman who became his wife, only to leave him and his precious daughter behind.

He would not take a single step toward that mistake again. His daughter and career were too important. But he wasn't about to throw Astrid under the bus. She was a capable partner in her work, leaving him with no choice but to remove himself from the equation. It was a sacrifice he had to make to save his own skin.

"You can't be serious," Astrid said in reply to his assertion that they didn't make a good team. "We work together so well. We made it through the first round on the Seaport project and don't forget, that was on a very tight timeline."

"What was that I heard about Seaport? Are you two talking shop?" Grant turned and stepped into the middle of their conversation.

Clay had planned on speaking to Grant about this in a private meeting on Monday morning, not launching into it in front of anyone else, especially not Astrid. "We were, actually. I'm wondering if I can be taken off the project, so I can shift to some of the more pressing jobs we have ahead."

A deep crease formed between Grant's eyes. "I thought you were enjoying it. And it's such a high profile assignment. I would think that with the Architect of the Year nomination, this is your time to step into the spotlight, not out of it."

Tara had apparently overheard and excused herself from the person she'd been chatting with. Clay wanted to disappear into himself. He never should have allowed this to be discussed in the middle of a cocktail party. It was stupid and foolish and entirely too public. Clay was a deeply private person. He'd always been that way.

"Everything okay over here?" Tara asked.

"Clay wants to be taken off the Seaport project." Grant slipped his arm around Tara's waist, but he still seemed deeply concerned.

"No. Absolutely not. You and Astrid are the dream team. Plus, now that I'm officially stepping into my role as co-CEO, I need you two to steer the ship on that project. I'm planning on handing Astrid all of the work I've been doing."

If only Tara knew that she was only making his argument that much stronger. She'd at least been a bit of a buffer between Astrid and him. Now she was leaving it to just the two of them? "The project right now is nothing more than adapting the existing plan to meet the city's needs. Those are small details that are best left to one of the more junior architects." Clay hoped this new line of thinking would convince them.

Tara shook her head and pinched her lower lip between her fingers. "I don't know." She turned to Grant. "I would just feel a whole lot better about things if Clay was still the principal. He's been working on it from the very beginning. It would make me very nervous to step away from it if he wasn't still there."

Clay could not catch a break here. He kept losing ground, despite having dug in his heels.

"It's my fault," Astrid interjected, surprising the hell out of Clay. "The truth is that Clay has a hard time working with me. But don't worry. I will do better. We will work out our difficulties and everyone can proceed with their plans. Don't worry about it."

Tara returned her sights to Astrid, then directed them at Clay. "Is that what this is really about? Office politics?"

"There's more to it than that," Clay answered.

"Do you want to tell me what, exactly?" Tara countered.

As for further explanation, Clay had none. It looked as though his bed had been made for him and he'd better learn to lie down in it, however much it bothered him. Perhaps he could start wearing blinders to the office or tell Astrid that they should only communicate via email. "Look, it's my fault. Not Astrid's. I'm too rigid in my ways." He didn't want to cast himself in a bad light, but he also didn't want Astrid to take the heat for this. He'd started it.

"Give us some time," Astrid said. "We'll work it out. And if we don't, I'll take myself off the project."

A frustrated grumble fought to leave Clay's throat. That wasn't what he wanted either. But he didn't really have a choice. He could live with the torment of Astrid for another week or two, then he'd figure out his next move. "Yes. Fine. We'll find a compromise."

"Okay, then," Grant said, seeming satisfied. He and Tara were quickly whisked back into the flow of the party, celebrating their many bits of good news.

Clay knew he was supposed to be happy tonight. He had the nomination he'd worked hard for. And if things were simpler for him, he could allow himself to feel at least a little jubilation. He might even flirt with Astrid, or at the very least, not let her get to him so much.

"I hope I didn't put you on the spot," Astrid said. "I just don't want things to be strained between us." She looked down at her feet, then back up, capturing him with the storm in her eyes. "I mean, any more than they are."

Good God, he was a jerk. Part of him wanted to explain what his problem really was, but even he failed to fully comprehend it. He only knew that there was a force deep inside him telling him to stay away. It was a reflex. He couldn't help it. "I'll see you at the office on Monday, okay?"

"I'd like to have a meeting first thing so we can talk about this some more."

He shook his head. "No need for a conversation. It's not you. It's me." He pulled his keys out of his pocket. He needed to get out of there, get back to his daughter, Delia, and sleep off the effects of this night. Perhaps he'd have a clearer head in the morning. He scanned the crowd for his sister, but she was nowhere to be seen. He'd text her when he got home. "Have a good weekend," he said to Astrid before starting for the door.

"There's no way it's just you." Astrid was right behind him, trotting along in her heels, the ones that made her legs look unbelievable.

"Trust me. It is." He pulled the door open, but out of habit, he stood aside for Astrid. Damn his gentlemanly ways.

Astrid turned back to him as soon as she was out on the flagstone landing. The night breeze blew her hair across her face, and she shook it free. He struggled to remain standing. How could any woman be so beautiful? "It's never just one person's fault. And I know there has to be a reason you treat me the way you do."

Clay had worried his cold shoulder had gotten to be too much. He closed the door behind him. "I'm sorry if I haven't been the most fun to work with. I'm under a lot of stress. It's not an excuse, but it might explain some of it."

"I know I can be overly enthusiastic. I'm just excited to have a job where I feel like I have more of a purpose. I was a model for years and that didn't make me feel very valuable."

"I'm sure your employers were very happy with your work." How could they not be? She was so damn sexy, she could sell a brick to a man standing on a diving board. He resumed his trek to his car.

"Maybe. I don't really know. But I do know that I enjoy being at Sterling and I don't want that to change."

"You own a chunk of the company. You can write your own ticket, can't you?" He stopped and turned to her. "Honestly, do you even need to work?"

"Do you?" She artfully arched both eyebrows at him.

No, he didn't need to work, at least not for the money. He and Miranda had inherited the entire family fortune when their grandmother died. But he did need to work for his own sanity. It kept his mind occupied. It kept him from constantly rehashing his past. "How do you know that?"

"I ask questions."

Clay did not want anyone digging around for information about him. That didn't sit well with him at all. "Well, don't. You and I are coworkers. There's no reason for you to know anything about my personal life." Anger was bubbling up inside him. He just needed to get to his car.

"I'm sorry. I'm trying to understand."

"Understand what? Me?" He nearly started laughing. As far as he was concerned, he was an easy case. If he was left alone to live his life, he'd be fine.

"Yes, you." She gripped his elbow and her warmth traveled through his body at warp speed. "I want to be able to work with you. I want to learn from you, and collaborate, and try to soak up at least a little of your brilliance."

He stood paralyzed. He didn't know what he was supposed to say to that. She was so earnest, so unrelenting in her pursuit of a compromise. As far as he was concerned, that only made her more dangerous. Why couldn't she simply give up on him, go back inside, and forget about this whole thing?

"Why do you hate me, Clay? I'm struggling to understand what I did."

"I don't hate you." *It's that I can't stop thinking about you.*

"But it feels that way sometimes."

"I'm sorry. I don't know what else to say." He clicked the fob and strode double-time to his Audi, fumbling for the door handle like a fool. He wasn't going to let another woman get to him. Not like last time. Not ever again. He started the engine and the lights immediately came on. Straight ahead, Astrid stood there, shaking her head in disbelief. Even in the harshest light he could imagine, she was beautiful and alluring and the exact woman he wanted to take in his arms and kiss. She was also so difficult to understand. What could make someone so eager to trust in a virtual stranger?

He'd learned long ago to trust in virtually no one.

Two

A peace offering was in order for Monday morning. Astrid decided that hers would be simple—baked goods. Clay displayed no weakness for anything, but he did sometimes duck out of the office in the morning for a doughnut from the bakery across the street from Sterling Enterprises. Was satiating his sweet tooth the way out of the dog house with Clay? Astrid wasn't sure, but it couldn't hurt to try.

The line was always long. Sometimes it was out the door, but this morning, Astrid must have been lucky, because that wasn't the case. She took her place in the bustling, lively space, where six or seven people worked the counter, taking orders, ringing up customers, bagging pastries and making lattes.

Heavenly smells of cinnamon, chocolate, coffee and steamed milk swirled in the air. It was a warm and cozy spot, which did make Astrid wonder about Clay. People got a sliver of happiness here—is that why he liked to come? Or did he feel out of place?

Astrid knew very well what it was like to feel that way, starting with her family. She was the youngest of six, and the only girl. One could argue that she'd been out of place from the word *go*. Her mother had apparently always wanted a girl, but her father had been opposed to the idea of more children. There were already plenty of mouths to feed and their four-bedroom house in Bergen, on the southwestern coast of Norway, was bursting at the seams.

Astrid's five brothers were all tall, strapping young men, who not only treated Astrid as though she were made of glass, but also acted as though she might be an alien. She'd had to fight for their attention, and most important, to be included. They all had their lives pretty well worked out when Astrid came along. She was the intruder, the one who disrupted the family equilibrium. It didn't help that her mother, who was loving and full of heart, was always nagging her brothers to take her along when they went places and let her be included in their activities. It wasn't until she had a growth spurt at age eleven and convinced her oldest brother to let her play football with them that she finally earned some respect. She'd gotten pretty roughed up that day, but she'd stood nearly shoulder to shoulder with them and she'd competed. She'd forced them to include her.

Astrid couldn't ignore the parallel here, with Clay not wanting her around and Tara taking the role of her mom, urging them to find a way. But Astrid was not a little girl, she was a grown woman, and she owned just as much of the company as Tara did. She would sort this out for herself. She didn't need anyone else's help. She just needed doughnuts.

When she finally reached the front of the line, she was pleased to see they still had several of Clay's favorite, the Diego, filled with dark chocolate custard and topped with caramelized sugar like crème brûlée. She ordered three, two for Clay and one for herself. She might as well see what all the fuss was about. As she was waiting for her coffee, a familiar face caught her eye—Sandy, a woman who'd worked at Sterling as a general assistant when Astrid first arrived. Sandy was a valuable member of the support staff, confident and capable. Sandy had also essentially disappeared.

As she approached the door, Astrid eyed her, unsure if she'd identified her correctly. When the woman caught sight of Astrid and quickly looked away, Astrid knew she had to say something. "Sandy? Is that you?"

She turned, confirming Astrid's suspicions. "Oh. Hello, Ms. Sterling. How are you?"

"Good. I'm on my way into the office." Astrid held up the bag of doughnuts. "I have to say that we miss you. We were all a bit puzzled about the way you left. You didn't say goodbye. You didn't even give any notice. It was quite a scramble before the first deadline on the Seaport project."

All color had drained from Sandy's face. Apparently she wasn't used to being called out on things, but Astrid had no reason to be anything less than up front about it. "I know. It wasn't my finest moment. I got pulled away by a second job. I didn't want to tell anyone, but I was moonlighting a bit at the time. San Diego can be so expensive."

"Yes, it can be. Weren't you being paid well at Sterling?"

"I was. I definitely was. It's just that my other employer and I have a long history." She shifted back and forth on her feet, seeming uncomfortable. "I owed my boss a favor, and he wanted me to work on a project and wouldn't take no for an answer. It's a long story."

Astrid nodded, realizing this might be as much as she'd ever learn about this. "I see. Well, I hope it all got straightened out."

Sandy shrugged. "I ended up getting let go, actually."

"So you left Sterling for nothing?"

Sandy nodded sheepishly. "It was so stupid."

Astrid drew a deep breath in through her nose. "We've filled your position, but do you have my number? Call me if you don't end up finding anything. Maybe there's something we can do."

"Thank you, Ms. Sterling. I'll do that."

"Sandy, do you mind me asking you what your other employer does?"

"Just more real estate development, but nothing in California. They're based in Seattle."

Seattle and real estate development made Astrid think of her ex-husband's estranged brother, but surely there were a lot of companies like that in Washington state. "Well, good luck with everything. And call me if you find yourself still looking for a job."

Astrid strode out of the bakery and made her away across the street, taking the elevator up to the Sterling offices. As was always the case, especially on a Monday morning, it was buzzing with activity. She bid her good mornings to coworkers as she filed through the maze of halls to Clay's office. His door was open, but her heart still flipped at the thought of looking inside. Just the idea of seeing him and offering a pastry made her nervous. It wasn't right. This was a professional setting. They were adults. She had to stop acting like a fool.

When she peeked inside, she realized that seeing him wasn't the problem. *Not* seeing him was. *Dammit. He's not here yet.* She stepped inside his office and flipped on the light. It wasn't like Clay to be late for work. Astrid really hoped he hadn't decided to resign over the weekend. He didn't like her much, but he didn't really hate her to that extent, did he?

She drew in a deep breath, weighing her options. She didn't want to wait too long and appear truly desperate. The only answer was to leave the doughnuts and a note. At least if he wasn't pleased by the gesture, she didn't have to witness his reaction. Grabbing a piece of paper from the credenza, she scribbled out a note.

I thought you might enjoy some of your favorite doughnuts.
—Astrid

She stared at what she'd written, realizing it was all wrong. Only someone who had been very carefully watching him would know what his favorite doughnut was. This was quite possibly the stupidest idea ever. She folded up the paper, stuffed it in her pants pocket and plucked the bakery bag from his desk. Just as Clay walked in.

"Uh. Good morning?" He looked as confused as could be.

If Astrid thought her heart was misbehaving earlier, it was now up to no good, thundering away in her chest. "Good morning." God, he looked good in his charcoal-gray suit. It was well-cut for his broad shoulders and towering stature, but Astrid had always noticed that it was a little snug on his arms. That suit couldn't hide whatever glorious muscles were under there. It could only flaunt them.

Clay cleared his throat and walked behind Astrid to his desk. "Is there something I can help you with?"

Astrid realized that she had no choice but to come clean. "I brought you doughnuts. I know you like them." Dead silence followed her admission, which made her feel even more stupid.

"I forgot to eat this morning, so thank you." He set down his laptop case.

Astrid hadn't realized she'd been holding her breath, waiting for a blip of positivity from him. Finally, she could exhale. She presented the bag, then remembered that they weren't all for him. "Actually, one of those is mine."

The smallest of smiles crossed his lips, which sent zaps of electricity through her. She immediately began conspiring, wondering what she could do next to bring about another grin. "You don't seem like a person who would like sweets," he said.

She opened the paper sack and fished out one of the doughnuts, then handed the bag over to Clay. "Are you kidding? Anything sweet is fun. I'm fun." She peeled back the parchment partially wrapped around the pastry and took a big bite. Chocolate custard oozed out at the corners of her lips, but she was so overcome with how delicious it was, she didn't care. "Wow. That is so good."

"I know. Right?" He went in for his own taste, his eyes drifting shut for a moment.

Astrid had to steel herself as she watched the blissful look cross his face. First a smile then this. She might start buying doughnuts every day. "Did you oversleep this morning?"

"Huh?" He licked a bit of custard from his thumb, making her light-headed.

"You said you didn't have time for breakfast."

"No. My daughter. She wanted her hair a certain way for school and she's not quite able to do it herself." He wiped his hands with a napkin, then held them up. "Obviously these things aren't good at braids or whatever it was that she wanted. I'm not sure I even know how to properly operate a barrette."

Astrid had admired Clay's hands from the moment she first met him in this office. They were big and strong, but deft when he showed his architectural brilliance and drafted by hand. Now that she had the wholly adorable image of Clay and his young daughter having a spat over her hair, his hands were now enticing in a whole new way. "You don't talk about your daughter very often. How old is she? What's her name?"

"I don't want to talk about her at work."

"You brought her up, not me."

"And now I'm asking you to not talk about her."

He was so infuriating. "Okay, but if you ever need help with her hair, I'm happy to come over. Braids are very traditional in Norway, so I know how to do them dozens of different ways."

"No, thanks." He cleared his throat and averted his eyes. "I can figure it out on my own."

And just like that, Astrid felt as though she were back at square one. Apparently, she could only offer

Clay so much niceness at one time. Too much and he would cut her off. "Okay. Whatever you say."

Clay hadn't meant to shut down Astrid's offer to help with his daughter's hair so quickly. It was a reflex. He would do anything to protect Delia, and that meant keeping everyone he didn't fully trust away from her. What if Astrid came over and Delia became attached, and then Astrid flitted back to Norway or decided one day that she no longer had time for his daughter? Clay couldn't subject Delia to that kind of rejection. Delia had already suffered the ultimate rebuke when her own mother had left them. He would not let anyone come close to hurting her like that again.

"You're a smart guy. I'm sure you'll figure it out," Astrid said. "I guess I'll take my doughnut and head back to my office."

Clay felt like such an ass. Astrid hadn't done anything other than be her usual sweet self. Why did he have to be so wary of kindness? "Thank you for that. It was nice."

"I'm trying to make our working relationship a little better."

Now he felt even worse, but he also knew that she was missing the point. The more wonderful she tried to be, the more drawn he was to her. And the more tempted he felt by her, the more dangerous she became. He would not put his heart on the line again. He couldn't do it. "Don't feel like you need to do anything outside the normal course of our professional interactions. It's not necessary."

Astrid stopped at his doorway and turned back to him. She was wearing a simple black dress today, one that showed off her slender curves and made the deep brown of her eyes even more intense. He couldn't see a single flaw in her, and he'd spent plenty of time looking for one, hoping he could assign a reason to not be so attracted to her. He'd failed.

"What's not necessary?" Tara appeared at the entrance to Clay's office.

"I brought Clay a doughnut this morning. He was just telling me why I didn't need to do that." Astrid shot him a look that was born of pure annoyance. It was so ridiculously hot that everything in his body went tight.

"So I take it neither of you had a chance to cool off this weekend?" Tara stepped inside and sat on the small sofa in his office. Astrid joined her, perching on the arm and crossing her legs.

Cool off? Clay needed an ice bath after even five minutes with Astrid, especially right now when she was distracting him by letting her black pump dangle from her foot. "All I said was that she shouldn't go out of her way to be nice to me."

Tara shook her head slowly. Now he had two women displeased with him. "Grant and I talked about it and we think the only way for you two to get past your troubles is to spend more time together."

Clay's stomach sank. "Wait. What?"

Tara held up her hand. "Hold on a minute. Hear me out. We think some time together outside the office would be a good idea. You both work incredibly hard and we think that the stress of the Seaport project has likely been the main reason you got off to a rocky start."

"I think there's more to it than that..." Clay wished there wasn't such a distinct edge of panic in his voice. It wasn't a good look.

Astrid let out a frustrated grumble. "Did you have something specific in mind, Tara?"

Clay was consumed by a flurry of silent wishes. *Please no spa retreats or trust falls or anything involving a beach or Astrid in a bathing suit.*

"I was specifically thinking the Architect of the Year Award ceremony in LA. You should go together. It will give Astrid a chance to meet more people in our industry, and it will give you two a chance to connect outside the office."

"But that's next weekend," Astrid blurted.

Finally, someone else in the room was willing to help him put on the brakes. "Exactly," Clay said.

"What's your objection, Astrid?" Tara asked.

"I need to find a dress."

Tara eyed Astrid. "You and I both know you will have zero problem finding a dress in time for you two to leave for LA. I'll go shopping with you. We can invite Miranda and talk business at the same time."

Astrid lips curled into a smile. "That sounds great."

"This will be good for Sterling, too. Clay has an excellent chance of winning, and it would be nice if he wasn't standing there by himself if he does."

Clay drew in a resigned breath through his nose. He had planned on going alone, but that was only because he was filled with existential dread over the ceremony. He desperately wanted to win, but he didn't want anyone to feel as though they needed to assuage his disappointment if he didn't. It was simply easier to be there on his own. "I guess I see what you're saying."

"It's settled then," Tara said. "I'll get my assistant to book an extra room at the hotel for Astrid."

"Okay," Astrid said.

"And I take it you're all set with a babysitter for Delia?" Tara asked.

"Miranda is taking her for the night. Those two adore each other, so it won't be a problem."

"Perfect. I'll let Grant know this is all settled. Where are we at with Seaport?"

"We're digging into the more detailed changes the city requested and coordinating with the landscape designers for their side of the project," Astrid said. "I estimate we're ahead of schedule for the next presentation in mid-November."

"Good. That will allow for any mistakes," Tara said.

Clay suddenly found it hard to swallow. He had made the crucial gaffe on site orientation for the first proposal. It had almost cost them the project, and

Clay was committed to never having another misstep like that one. "It won't happen again."

Tara got up from the couch and made her way for the door. "Still, it's nice to have a little wiggle room."

Clay dropped down into his office chair, and he and Astrid sat in silence for several moments after Tara left. They both seemed equally stunned and unsure, as if Clay needed another means of feeling more connected to Astrid.

"I wasn't expecting that," she finally said.

"Me neither."

"If you don't want me to go, I won't. Even if you want me to tell Tara at the last minute that I'm sick or something. It's your night and I don't want to ruin it."

Clay's shoulders dropped. Would this feeling of being torn in two ever go away? "I had envisioned being on my own, but it might be nice to have some company."

"Might?"

"I don't know, Astrid. I don't know how you are in a situation like that. I'm already plenty nervous about it. This is a professional accolade I've worked very hard for. It means a lot to be recognized and I know I'm going to be pretty worked up about it that night. Maybe you don't like being around someone who's so on edge."

Astrid unleashed a light and musical titter that filled the room.

"What's so funny?"

"Clay, you are always on edge. Always. And I

don't know you that well, but I suspect it's because you spend a little too much time in your own head."

She wasn't wrong, but he wasn't about to admit it. "What's your point?"

"My point is that I'm already used to handling you at your worst. And I've attended more award ceremonies than you can possibly imagine. I have no problem putting on a beautiful dress and walking the red carpet. I can do it in my sleep."

Of course she could. Her modeling career had put her in untold glamorous settings. Surely dozens of men had made their overtures to Astrid, and she'd had her pick of the lot. It was one more reason to keep his brain on this very narrow path he'd carved out for them—the one where they were colleagues and nothing else, regardless of his attraction to her. Clay didn't know her romantic history, but he could imagine a long string of broken hearts in her wake. He wasn't about to be the next.

"And more than anything, I'm very good in a crisis," Astrid added. "So if you panic or get too nervous, I'm sure I can find something to distract you."

He already knew she'd have no problem doing that. But maybe this wasn't the worst idea. It was a work trip and nothing else. He could introduce her to some people, and it would be nice to not be alone after the winner was announced—good news or bad, he was sure he'd need a steady hand to hold on to. "Okay. As long as you're good with it."

Astrid rose from her spot on the couch. "Of course

I am. I like the idea of being someone's insurance policy."

"What do you mean by that?"

Astrid smoothed the front of her dress. "I mean that even if you lose, I don't think anyone will be feeling sorry for you."

Clay swallowed hard as he watched her walk out of his office. This was going to be a test unlike any he'd experienced in quite some time. He picked up his phone and pulled up Miranda on speed dial.

"Hey. This is a surprise," she said when she answered.

"I was hoping you and I could talk one night this week."

"Sounds serious."

"I need some advice about how to ignore my attraction to a woman."

"No way. I'm not doing that. I want you to pay attention if you're attracted to someone."

Clay sat back in his chair and cradled his forehead in his hand. "Yeah. That's not going to happen."

Three

Clay arrived at Miranda's house Thursday night around six with his daughter, Delia, in tow.

"My two favorite people," Miranda announced as she threw open the door.

"Aunt Miranda!" Delia exclaimed, bounding inside and into his sister's waiting arms.

Clay smiled as he watched the pair embrace. They had quite a lot in common, both with long dark hair, big brown eyes and of course, him wrapped around their little fingers. There had been a time, when he and Miranda were young, that he never would have dared to imagine such a loving scene in his future. The day their mother dropped them off with their grandmother, never to return, was the start of their treacherous past. The details of that day would always be murky for Clay, who had only been five years old, but Miranda, who had been only two, didn't remember it at all. One thing Clay did clearly recall was the feeling of losing all hope, and the fierce need to protect Miranda at all costs. They'd stood there together, holding hands, looking at a stern and cold woman they hardly knew, who was suddenly about to rule their whole world.

He stepped inside the foyer and closed the door behind them. "Delia, do you want to go look at the aquarium?" Miranda had a large tropical tank in her home office, stocked full of live coral and dozens of colorful fish.

"Can I?" Delia asked.

"Of course," Miranda answered, laughing as Delia skittered off. "You want a drink? Somebody might as well enjoy a glass of wine since I can't." Miranda pressed her hand to her pregnant belly, which was only a slight protrusion. She was a little shy of four months along, so that would soon change. Single parenthood was another life detail Miranda and Clay shared now. Miranda had been about to announce the pregnancy to her husband, Johnathon, on the day he was killed by a line drive on the golf course.

"No, thank you. I'm fine." He wanted to keep a clear head when discussing Astrid, plus he needed to drive Delia home. "How are you feeling?"

"Good, but definitely like my stomach is starting to pooch out. I already have a little bump."

Clay slung his arm around his sister's shoulder. "I didn't want to say anything, but..."

Miranda gently elbowed him in the ribs. "You're welcome to keep your mouth shut, mister. Come on. Let's go sit in the living room." She led the way, taking the end of one of the comfortable sectional couches. "So, you wanted to talk? We should probably do it now while Delia is in the other room."

Clay found himself feeling uncertain about discussing the topic of Astrid with his sister, but he knew he could trust Miranda with his life, so if he had any chance of setting his mind straight about this, she was his best shot. "It's Astrid."

Miranda narrowed her eyes, seeming confused. "Okay. And we're not talking about your work relationship?"

"Yes and no. It's a mix of work and personal and I don't know how to deal with it."

"You're going to have to be a lot more specific or I can't help you at all." Miranda's eyes lit up as if she was putting it all together. "You two aren't involved, are you?" she whispered.

"No. We aren't. But if our situation was completely different and if I didn't have Delia to think about or have any worries about the past repeating itself, I might want to be." He felt foolish to make that admission, like he was a teenager. Why did Astrid make him so unsure of himself?

"Interesting." Miranda sat back, seeming satisfied with the leap she'd taken.

"What?"

"I've been wondering when you would finally want to get out there again. It's been four years since the divorce, so I guess the timing is about right."

"No. That's not what this is. I am not out anywhere. Not at all."

"Then why don't you tell me what it is?"

He sighed heavily and just came out with it. "I can't stop thinking about her." He went on to explain that he was hopelessly attracted to Astrid, and not just because she was beautiful, but because everything she did only seemed to confirm that she was too good to be true. Clay reminded Miranda that he had fallen prey to that very idea when he met his ex-wife, Delia's mom. Of course, Miranda had been there for the whole disaster. She'd helped him pick up the pieces. "I asked to be taken off the Seaport project, just in the hopes that distance would make it easier to stay away from her. But Tara and Grant disagreed, and now they want the two of us to attend the Architect of the Year awards together."

"I heard."

"You did?"

Miranda nodded. "Yep. She wants Tara and me to go dress shopping with her. I'd say your plan backfired."

"Spectacularly." He laughed quietly, trying not to take this situation too seriously. "You've spent more time with Astrid than I have. What do you think of her?"

"You do realize this is an odd situation for me to comment on, right? She was married to Johnathon before I was. I see why men would be attracted to her, but I don't like to think about it too much."

Clay could appreciate that he'd put his sister in an awkward spot. "Fair enough. I get it."

"I don't really know what you want me to say anyway. Are you asking for my blessing?"

"No. I was hoping you would tell me that I'm right to want to stay away from her. At least as far as anything outside our professional relationship."

"Well, I don't know her that well. I'd like to think that Johnathon would never have married a woman who was anything less than amazing and wonderful, but I don't know for sure, and no person is perfect. Everyone has faults. And we might have mutual interests in Sterling Enterprises, but I don't trust her unconditionally."

Somehow, these negatives weren't nearly the comfort Clay had hoped they might be. "Okay. That's good to know."

"But…"

Clay hadn't bargained on a *but*.

"I do trust her somewhat," Miranda continued. "There's something about her that makes you want to give her whatever she asks for."

It was as if his sister had pulled the words straight out of his mouth. "Yes. How does she do that?"

"I don't know. Although I will say that she has a good heart. She had every reason to be horribly

jealous of my pregnancy. She and Johnathon suffered through years of infertility. That's what drove
them apart."

"It did?" This was the first he'd heard about the
conditions under which Johnathon and Astrid had
split up.

"Yes. She wanted a baby with Johnathon and I'm
the one who got what she didn't." Miranda's sights
fell to her belly.

"I had no idea."

"She doesn't exactly go around chatting about that
part of her life. She might be very open, but some
things are too painful to share." Miranda sat a little
straighter and reached for Clay's hand. "She's been
very sweet to me about the baby. She didn't even
hesitate to congratulate me when she found out. That
takes a big heart. And I'd like to think that anyone
with such a generous nature would be a good person
to fall in love with."

Clay nearly laughed. "That's a pretty big leap.
I'm not going to fall in love with Astrid. I'm just not.
That's not in the cards for me."

"Why not? Why do you keep clinging to this idea
that you'll never find love again? It makes me so
sad."

"Daddy," Delia called from the other room.
"Come watch the fish with me and do the thing
where you make the funny voices."

Clay gestured over his shoulder with a nod.
"That's why. Delia is my life. I can't let a woman

come into our lives and get close to her and then leave again. It wouldn't just kill me, it would hurt her. I need to worry about her, too."

"I still think you have to take that risk at some point. If you're going to have a full life, you might need to take the leap."

"You, Delia, and my job are my life. That's enough for me. There's no reason to get my heart squashed again." He got up from the couch, but Miranda stuck out her leg to stop him.

"Hold on a second."

"What?"

"I just want you to promise me one thing."

Clay dropped his head to one side, knowing that whatever she was about to say would likely make his life more difficult. "What's that?"

"Promise me that you will at least be open to the idea that love might find you again. It doesn't have to be with Astrid and it doesn't have to be right now. You don't even have to be open all the way. Just a little bit. I hate the idea that one person hurt you and you aren't willing to try again."

"I'm not sure that advice helps me for my trip to LA with Astrid."

"For that, I want you to have fun. You've worked too hard for too long not to simply enjoy the ride."

Miranda had officially not helped him get anywhere with his thinking, but she wasn't responsible for his inability to see clearly on this matter. "I'll try to keep that in mind."

"Daddy!" Delia ran back into the room with a look of pure concern. "I'm waiting."

Clay couldn't help but smile at Delia. "I know. I'm coming."

"Clay? One more question," Miranda said.

"What's that?"

"Any thoughts on which direction I should point Astrid in when I go dress shopping with her?" Miranda got up from the couch and rounded it to face him.

Clay couldn't begin to formulate an answer to this question. "I have no earthly idea. Surprise me."

Miranda snickered. "I'd be careful what you wish for."

Most people probably assumed that a former model would live to shop for clothes. The truth was that Astrid saw it as a necessary evil, especially with her job, where she needed to look the part of capable businesswoman. Attending the awards ceremony with Clay would require a far different look than was appropriate for the office. She was relieved she was going to have Tara and Miranda on hand to be her sounding board.

She met them downtown at Ruby, an exclusive high-end boutique, early Friday evening. The store manager, Cherise, had a bottle of champagne on ice for Tara and Astrid, and for Miranda, she'd brought in a smoothie from a juice bar nearby and sparkling water. Cherise had also taken much of the deliberation out of this process by pulling two dozen dresses from their extensive selection, after speaking with Astrid on the phone and finding out the nature of the event and what Astrid wanted.

Tara and Miranda set their purses on a brilliant fuchsia velvet settee. Above them, chandeliers dripped with crystals and provided soft lighting, while a plush white carpet beneath their feet made every step feel luxurious. The three of them began the process of perusing the gowns the manager had selected.

"What sort of look are you going for?" Tara asked.

Astrid glanced at Cherise. This had been a difficult thing for Astrid to put into words during their phone conversation. "Classic. Beautiful. Tasteful. But still sexy." Astrid pinched her thumb and index finger together. "A little sexy. Nothing too over the top."

"Smart. You'll be in a room full of nerdy architects. You don't need anyone fainting or going into cardiac arrest," Tara said.

Astrid laughed. "That wasn't my worry. I was thinking more about professionalism."

"You don't want to play it too safe and look like you walked straight out of the office." Miranda chose a slinky black gown from the rack. "How about this?"

Astrid considered the dress, which had a very low neckline and an especially slim silhouette. If she'd been going for full-on seduction, it would have been a no-brainer. But this was a work trip and Astrid intended to dress accordingly. "I think that might be too sexy." Plus, she didn't want to be the center of attention that night. It was Clay's accomplishment. She was his support system. But still, she could imagine the silky fabric draping her bare skin, and what it might feel like to stand next to him while wearing it. Every nerve ending in her body would come to life, a torment she wasn't sure she could endure. To feel that sexy while with the man she couldn't get out of her head, when she knew that it was in everyone's best interests to keep things professional? That would be a waste of a perfectly beautiful dress.

"What about this?" Tara offered another choice, a simple off-white strapless gown.

"Elegant, but don't you think that's a little bridal?"

That turned Miranda's head. "If anything is going to terrify my brother, it's a wedding dress."

Astrid had wondered about the fate of Clay's marriage to his daughter's mother but had been understandably terrified to ask him. She only knew that he was divorced. "Was it that bad?"

"Yes. She ripped my brother's heart out and walked all over it with the wardrobe of Louboutin and Jimmy Choo shoes she bought after cleaning out one of his investment accounts and subsequently moving to the Maldives." Miranda rolled her eyes. "Like she needs all those heels in a place where there's nothing but beaches."

Astrid was floored. She had no idea it had been

so dreadful. Was that part of the reason Clay was so closed off? "How could a woman do that? And leave behind her child?"

Miranda shook her head in disbelief. "I have no idea. I mean, I'm sure my brother is not easy to be married to, but he was devoted to her and he would do anything for Delia. I don't know what else she could have possibly wanted from him."

Astrid felt as though her heart was being tugged from her chest to her throat. The thought of what Clay had been through was so sad. "That's so awful. I feel terrible for him."

"Me too," Tara added. "Every time I hear that story, it sounds more and more unbelievable."

"Oh, it happened," Miranda said. "I was there for the aftermath and trust me, it was not pretty."

"Hence the fear of wedding gowns," Tara said.

"Precisely." Miranda returned her attention to the rack of dresses. "Let's get back to a topic that's a bit more fun. Like finding you the perfect gown."

A few more minutes of browsing and they decided on three options, then Astrid went into the fitting room to try them on. The first two were instantly rejected by Tara and Miranda. One was deemed too drab and the other too ill-fitting. With less than a week until they left for the ceremony, there was no time for major alterations. Astrid tried on the final option, an off-the-shoulder navy blue gown with a fitted bodice and full skirt. It was absolutely gorgeous and struck the perfect balance between professional and sexy.

"I think this is the one." Astrid zipped open the curtain and emerged from the fitting room.

Tara and Miranda looked at Astrid, then at each other. "Yes. That's it," they said in unison.

"It's perfect," Miranda added. "My brother is a lucky guy to have you as his date that night."

"It's not a date," Astrid quickly followed.

Miranda cleared her throat. "Right. Of course."

Astrid took one more look at herself in the full-length mirror. When she swished the skirt, she realized there was a high slit hidden in the folds. "Do you think this is okay?" she asked, kicking it open.

"With your legs?" Tara asked. "Yes."

Astrid smiled and shook her head, then retreated into the dressing room, relieved this much was decided. She didn't want to think about it anymore. She changed back into her regular clothes and asked Cherise to ring up the dress. Then she took a seat with Tara and Miranda.

"I wanted to ask you both about something. Johnathon's brother, Andrew, has a development firm up in Seattle, right?"

"He does," Miranda answered. "Why?"

Astrid pressed her lips together, wondering if she was pulling at seemingly random threads. "Tara, do you remember Sandy? She was already working at Sterling when I started."

"Of course I do," Tara answered. "She was on

staff when I started as well. In fact, Grant gave her the job of being my assistant on my first day. She'd been working with Johnathon and knew about his interest in the Seaport project. She was able to help us deal with the city."

"And then she disappeared. At the most inconvenient time as I remember."

Tara downed the last of her champagne and got up to pour herself another glass. "It was a total nightmare. She vanished on the Friday before the presentation. Grant and I spent all weekend trying to fix the mistake Clay made."

Astrid was still putting all of this together, but she was certainly suspicious that something wasn't quite right. "That's what always bothered me. The idea that Clay would miss a detail like the site orientation. I've worked with him for nearly two months now and he simply doesn't make errors like that."

"Anyone can mess up," Miranda said. "Even my brother, the control freak."

Astrid sighed. "Okay, well, here's the thing. I ran into Sandy the other day at the bakery across from the Sterling offices."

Tara's eyes grew impossibly large. "You did? Did you talk to her?"

"Of course I did. I wasn't going to leave without trying to find out what happened. She said that she'd been moonlighting while at Sterling. Then something about her other boss pulling her away. Something about owing him a favor. When I asked what the other company did, she said it was a development firm in Seattle." To Astrid's great surprise, the theory that had been tumbling around in her head didn't sound nearly as half-baked now that she'd had the guts to say it out loud. "That got me thinking about Andrew. He's in Seattle. He has a real estate development firm. He and Johnathon had been estranged for years. Andrew didn't even come to Johnathon's funeral."

"Right," Tara interjected. "And Grant and I ran into him in San Diego two weeks later, which seemed really odd to me. He could come to town for a baseball game, but he couldn't show up to pay his respects?"

Miranda shook her head. "I don't know where you two are going with this, but remember that Andrew reached out to me when he was here right after you and Grant saw him? He came over to the house. We had a very nice conversation. He was contrite and apologetic. He felt bad that he hadn't come to the funeral."

"So you don't think he's capable of interfering with Sterling?" Astrid asked.

"I think it's cute that you want to explain away my brother's mistake, but I really don't see how Andrew could possibly do anything like that," Miranda said. "What would Andrew get out of it, anyway? Silently tampering with a job? It seems like if he was trying to get even with Johnathon, he would have done something considerably more public. Now that Johnathon is gone, it seems even more unlikely."

"Maybe," Astrid said, gnawing on her finger. "You're probably right."

"How did you leave things with Sandy?" Tara asked.

"I told her that if she needed a job, she should call me. She was a great employee, even though she quit with no notice. And something told me not to burn that bridge."

Tara pursed her lips. "Let me know if she calls you."

"Oh, I will." Astrid's mind was swirling with the details. None of it seemed to add up. And maybe that was Miranda's point. Astrid's theory went nowhere and she needed to leave it alone.

Four

Clay wanted to believe that he saw things others couldn't. Possibilities. Potential. His sister Miranda, a gifted interior designer, was the same way. It was a talent they'd both seemingly been blessed with at birth, and according to their grandmother, they got it from their mom. Not that either Clay or Miranda was ever able to confirm this for themselves. She'd left them behind when they were still young.

This talent made Clay quite good at predicting how a situation would go. As much as he'd been thinking about the trip to LA for the Architect of the Year award, he had not seen it happening like this—Astrid in the passenger seat of his Bentley SUV, distracting him in every way imaginable. It was more than just her beauty and beguiling smell, a most intriguing mix of spring rain and vanilla. He'd trained himself to ignore a few of her more alluring qualities. But Astrid was a fidgeter. She couldn't sit still. She was constantly shifting her weight in her seat, adjusting the direction of the air vents in front of her, and straightening her clothes.

"Everything okay?" he asked, hoping there was some way to make it stop. He needed to keep his eyes trained on the road and she was drawing his attention every few seconds. If there was a problem, he desperately wanted to fix it. He was already on edge knowing the awards show was awaiting him that evening.

"It's not like you to ask how I'm doing," she quipped.

"And it's not like you to not offer a long-winded answer that somehow manages to weave in your entire life story."

A breathy burst of indignation left her lips, and she smacked his leg with the back of her hand. "You're so mean."

He couldn't help it, but the strike and her accusatory tone made him run about five degrees hotter. "I'm just being honest. You do like to tell people everything about everything."

"That's better than being so closed off. You don't tell anyone anything." She leaned forward and shot him a sideways glance with narrowed eyes. She had the most expressive face he'd ever seen, and of course, the most beautiful. "It's one of your most annoying qualities."

A corner of his mouth betrayed him by twitching with the beginnings of a smile. Astrid was normally so painfully kind that it felt as though he was dying a slow death. He liked it when she was being spirited and calling him out. He felt as though they were on a more even playing field. "If you want me to talk, I'll gladly share the things you do that drive me nuts." *Your chest heaves before you sigh, which is often. And you are constantly gathering your hair in your hands, twisting it, and pulling it over one shoulder, when all it does is fall back into place in a pleasing cascade of waves. And I see you laugh when you talk to other people, and your face lights up like the brightest sunrise. You never laugh when you're around me.*

"Just tell me. You can't hurt my feelings."

Oh, but he sensed that he could. She'd tried to play things off the night he attempted to quit the Seaport project, all under the guise of wanting to work through their problems, but he'd sensed that he was getting under her skin. It was the only thing that had made him back off. He knew she could hurt him, but he didn't have it in him to do the same to her. That was part of what made her such a dangerous, unknown quantity. "You ask a lot of questions. Personal questions."

"I'm trying to understand you. You are a puzzle."

"Do you think you can solve me?"

"I know I can. It might take some time, in part because you're hiding so many of the pieces."

He knew very well what she was getting at—she'd asked about Delia that day in the office when she'd brought him doughnuts and was trying to mend things between them. It had been an admirable attempt and he'd swatted it away, but she had no idea how deep his instinct was to protect Delia. "You asked about my daughter the other day. What do you want to know?"

"Is this a trick?" The thicker part of her Norwegian accent came out when she was particularly skeptical of something.

"No. I'm not saying I'll tell you everything, but you are free to ask."

"I don't know a thing. What's her name? How old is she?"

"Her name is Delia and she's five years old. She's in kindergarten."

"What is she like? Is she like you?"

"Are you asking if she's grumpy and no fun at parties? Because those would be odd qualities for a five-year-old."

She unleashed a quiet laugh, and it did something to him. It propped up his ego and made him want to try for more. "I meant is she brilliant? Is she very smart?"

He hadn't been prepared for that question at all, but he wasn't surprised that Astrid would pick up on everything, even the things he tried to downplay.

"She is exceptionally smart. I'm certain she'll eventually outpace me in that department."

"What does she like to do?"

"She loves books and playing outside. She's crazy about anything with a rainbow on it or that sparkles. She's very observant, so she likes to take it all in."

"Just like her dad."

"It's true. I do like rainbows."

Astrid burst into even more laughter, the musical tones filling the entire car. "That's not what I meant. I was talking about being observant. You love to sit back and watch. You study everything and then decide what to do."

"You aren't wrong." Her insight was uncanny, which was remarkable considering they'd only known each other for two months. He did do that, but it was simply his personality. He was far less likely to make a mistake if he took in all available information first before formulating a plan or making a decision. Being precise and measured always paid off. And the times when he hadn't done that, the times when he'd followed his heart without thinking too much, he'd ultimately paid a steep price.

"What about Delia's mother? Miranda told me a little bit about her. I'm so sorry."

Just like that, whatever happiness he was feeling about having this effortless back-and-forth with Astrid went up in thin air. He had to wonder what his sister had been thinking when she'd shared details of his personal life with Astrid. "Next topic." He didn't want to be cruel and cut her off, but he also didn't want to explain what had happened. How does a man go about illustrating the greatest rejection of his life? That would only lead to more questions. His marriage was contained in Pandora's box, and he wanted it kept closed.

"I knew I'd hit a dead end with you, eventually."

He had to turn this around—he couldn't take any more tension between them. Not with the nervousness of the awards show ahead. "What about you? Why don't you tell me more about you? I don't know much other than that you and my sister both married the same man."

"I thought I talked too much about me. That's basically what you said ten minutes ago."

"But what about your childhood? Your upbringing? You don't talk much about that at all. What were you like as a child?" He could imagine Astrid as the ingenue, sweet and girly, wearing pink dresses and dreaming up fantastical ideas in her head.

"I don't really like to talk about myself as a little girl. I did not have an easy childhood."

This was not something he'd anticipated. Astrid's generosity had made him assume that she'd had an easy upbringing and a nurturing home life. Where else could that have come from? And to think he'd always assumed they had little to nothing in common. "You don't have to talk about it if you don't want to."

She turned to him and he stole a quick glance, then returned his eyes to the road. Even in that split second, he saw an ocean of vulnerability in her eyes. It only made him want to save her from whatever hurt was bottled up inside her. "No. I will tell you. It's only fair, since you told me about Delia." She cleared her throat and wrapped her arms around her waist. "I am the youngest of six kids and the only girl in the family. I spent my entire childhood trying to get the attention of my father and brothers, but all they wanted to do was to push me aside to keep me safe."

"That doesn't sound so bad. It's natural for anyone to want to protect the most vulnerable member of the family. As the youngest and the only girl, I'm sure they saw you that way."

"I didn't want to spend my life on a high shelf, like a china teacup. All I ever wanted was to be included." She went on to explain that she used to dress like her brothers, in jeans and sweatshirts, and she begged them to let her play football with them. Her mother, who had wanted a sixth child only so they could try for a girl, had been hoping she could finally have a heavy dose of feminine trappings in the household after years of being the only woman, but Astrid wanted nothing to do with it. It caused friction with all members of the family.

"A lot of times, I felt like an intruder in my own home. I never belonged," she said, again shifting in her seat. "And that extended to school. The boys thought I was ugly and only a few of the girls wanted to be my friend."

"Ugly? You have got to be kidding." There wasn't an un-beautiful bone in Astrid's body. She was nothing less than pure grace and refinement, like she'd walked out of a portrait in a museum. "You must have just gone through an awkward phase. That happens to everyone."

"Until I was eighteen? That's a long time."

"What happened when you turned eighteen?"

"I went to university and figured out that if I stopped hiding under bulky sweaters, boys would pay attention to me."

Clay swallowed, finding it hard to get past the tightness in his throat. The thought of her revealing herself in the interest of drawing the male gaze did something to him. "But you became a model. You walked runways and were on the covers of magazines, right? That must have felt like a triumph. You showed them all that they were wrong."

She sucked in a deep breath and cast her sights out the window. "Maybe. But it didn't change who I was for all of the years before that happened. I still feel like that awkward girl a lot of the time."

"Even now?" If only she could see the way he saw her—flawless and composed. A woman to be admired, and quite possibly reckoned with.

"Even now." Astrid shifted in her seat again. "Honestly, your sister made me feel like that at first. It was hard to be around her and know that she was ultimately what my ex-husband wanted, all because I had fallen short of his expectations."

"Miranda was also robbed of her future with Johnathon, so I don't know how much there is in her situation to envy."

"She has his baby. That's no small thing." Astrid's voice cracked, and Clay felt as though the earth had shifted beneath him. The heartache Miranda had told him about was very real. And against his better judgment, there was a big part of him that wanted nothing more than to take all of it away.

Astrid swallowed back the emotion of her admission. Being vulnerable with Clay was far more difficult than it was with any other person she'd ever known. His tough outer shell was not only familiar, it was impenetrable. She knew the way he dismissed weakness and feelings as nothing more than a nuisance. She hoped he didn't think any less of her because she'd been willing to open up. The desire to keep him thinking the best of her was a strong one, with a fiercely beating heart and a need to survive. "We don't need to talk about me anymore. I want to know how you're feeling about tonight."

He noticeably tightened his grip on the steering wheel. It was another chance to admire his hands, just like she often found herself doing when they were in the office together. She especially loved to watch them in motion when he sketched up ideas before working them out on the computer. He openly admitted to being old-school and preferring paper and pencil to a mouse and a monitor. Just the thought of him employing some of that artistry and brilliance when putting his hands on her body was enough to make Astrid shudder. She couldn't imagine him ever wanting her like that.

"I'd be lying if I said I wasn't at least a little bit nervous. But I already told you that I would be."

"You must feel some certainty that you're going to win."

"I know nothing of the sort. The field of nominees is exceptionally talented. Men and women I deeply admire."

"I still think you'll win. And I think you know that, too." She didn't believe for a moment that he didn't know his own excellence.

"I don't."

"You're so confident. Everything you do at work is exact and deliberate. I often wonder how you can spend your whole day being so sure of yourself." It was the absolute truth and it amazed her that he might not actually see it. Astrid would have done anything to have one-tenth of the confidence he did.

"I am sure of my work. But that doesn't make it the best. It's only *my* best." He shrugged and exited the highway. Soon they were on Hollywood Boulevard, and then in the thick of Beverly Hills, with its wide boulevards and endless stream of luxury cars. This was a familiar landscape for Astrid. She had moved to Los Angeles after the grind of living in New York got to her. She'd yearned for wide open spaces and sunshine. Little had she known that she should have gone to San Diego for that. In LA, she'd mostly gotten bad traffic and fewer modeling jobs. But it was also where she met Johnathon, so she couldn't regret the move she'd made. It not only led her to the romance she'd never thought she would have, he opened up her whole world. Johnathon was fantastic at showing her the possibilities in life.

Clay pulled up in front of the Essex Beverly Hills Hotel. The bellman rushed to open Astrid's door as the valet rounded to Clay's side of the car. Astrid waited while he handed over the keys, then joined him as they walked inside. Astrid had stayed at five-star hotels all over the world, but it didn't make the lobby any less glamorous or beautiful, with a true old Hollywood feel. She loved being here with Clay, although what she really wanted to know was what it might be like to arrive with him, holding hands, as his partner. Instead, she was the tagalong, the woman who had been instructed by the company to attend.

They were greeted at the check-in desk by a female clerk who was, in Astrid's estimation, exceptionally pretty. Astrid couldn't help but notice that this didn't seem to register on Clay's radar. The realization made her feel a bit better about her own failure to capture his attention. Perhaps he was so focused on everything else in his life that women weren't even a passing thought. Was that because of his daughter's mother? Despite not knowing the full story of Clay's past, she thought there seemed to be considerable pain in that part of his life.

She wanted to know more. She longed to know it all, to at least have all of the pieces of the puzzle that was Clay Morgan so she could try to assemble them. The next twenty-four hours might be the only true chance she had to crack open his hard exterior and get to the root of what made him tick. She knew what he was like in the office—all business. And at most social events, at least back in San Diego, he was as distant from her as she could imagine. This was her window. If only he would let her in.

The clerk clacked away at her keyboard, then cocked her head to one side. "Mr. Morgan, I see you have a two-bedroom suite on your reservation. Is that correct?"

"No. It should be two rooms. Separate rooms."

The clerk returned to her computer, shaking her head from side to side. "I'm sorry, but I only see one room on your reservation, sir. It's a beautiful suite with two separate bedrooms and bathrooms. Will that be suitable? I'm afraid the rest of the hotel is booked for the state architecture commission's annual awards."

"Yes, I know that. That's why I'm here." He blew out an exasperated breath.

He was frustrated and Astrid saw no reason for it, other than his regular requests to be far away from Astrid. "It's fine, Clay. Really. It's fine. I'll stay on my side of the suite. You won't have to worry about me."

He turned to her with a pained expression on his face. "That's not what I'm saying. This just isn't what I expected."

"I'm very sorry, sir. The hotel will send up a bottle of champagne as a way of apologizing," the clerk said, offering two key cards.

"I don't think we need champagne."

"We do need the champagne. Thank you very much." Astrid took the cards from the woman. "Can you point us to the elevators?"

"Opposite side of the lobby."

"Thank you."

Astrid wasn't about to wait for Clay so he could further tell her why he was so disappointed to learn they'd been booked in the same room. She caught up with her at the elevator bank.

"I'm sorry," he said. "I just don't do well with surprises. And I guess the stress of the award show feels more real now that we're here."

Astrid slowly drew a breath through her nose, silently begging the universe for strength. "I understand. It'll all be fine." The elevator dinged and she stepped on board.

Clay and Astrid rode up to the top floor of the hotel. They wound their way around to their room, which was tucked away at the far end of the hall. Clay waved the key in front of the electronic lock and the light shined green. He opened the door, but held it for Astrid to enter first. She gladly accepted the chivalrous act from him. It felt like one of the few times he'd admitted that she was a woman and he was a man.

The room was just as elegant as the lobby downstairs, with a generous living area decorated in a color scheme of warm gold and cool gray with accents of black and white. "They've done a lovely job with the Hollywood Regency decor," she said. "It's all quite accurate to the period, as near as I can tell. Of course, I'm no expert. What do you think?"

"Do you know about Regency from when you lived in Los Angeles?"

Astrid set down her purse and padded over to the window to take in the view of the pool area below, ringed by palm trees, the water a pure blue. Now that it was fall, there were only a few guests sunning themselves in the slightly cooler temperatures. "I've been studying at night. I want to understand the art and architecture side of what we do at Sterling."

"Really?"

"Why? Does that surprise you?"

"To be honest, it does."

Astrid shot him a pointed glance. He looked so perfect, standing there with his hands stuffed into his pockets. All she wanted to do was to kiss him, if only to gather a few more pieces of the Clay Morgan puzzle. What would it be like? Would he want the same things she did? The questions sometimes kept her up at night. "I can't always get to sleep.

So I spend time researching these things. And I am truly interested. I know that you do more than design buildings to make money. I know you put a lot of attention into the process. I just want to understand how much."

He nodded, and Astrid scanned his face for some sign that she was softening him, but there was no real indication things were moving in that direction. "Well, good. I'm glad you're taking things at work so seriously."

"Does that make you feel like we might be better suited to work together than you previously thought?"

He pressed his lips together tightly. "The jury is still out on that. We're very different people."

Astrid felt as though everything with Clay was two steps forward, two steps back—the world's most frustrating cha-cha. "Sometimes different is good. It helps to see more than one point of view."

There was a knock at the door, giving Clay his excuse to take a break from their conversation. It was one bellman with their bags, and another wheeling a room service cart with champagne on ice, two glasses, and a plate of strawberries. If only she and Clay were there for romantic reasons…the mood would have been perfectly set.

Clay tipped the bellmen, then went to take their two hanging bags.

"Let me hang these for you," the bellman said. "The longer one is quite heavy."

"Heavy?" Clay asked.

Astrid waved the man in her direction, deciding she would take the bedroom on the farthest side of the suite. "Gowns are not light."

"I hope you didn't bring anything too extravagant," Clay called after her.

As if she needed more confirmation that he wanted her to stay buttoned up, professional, and platonic. "Trust me," she answered. "It's the exact right amount of extravagant."

The bellman snickered as he hung the garment bag in the closet for her. "Anything else I can do for you, ma'am?"

"Not unless you can figure out how to get my roommate to loosen up."

"The champagne?"

"Not a bad idea." Astrid led the way back into the living room and the bellmen departed, leaving Astrid and Clay all alone in their exquisite surroundings. She beelined for the bubbly. "A drink to take the edge off before we get dressed and head downstairs?"

Clay nearly lunged for the bottle, grasping her hand to stop her from peeling back the foil. "No. It's not a good idea."

"Why not?" She peered up at his handsome face, trying not to fixate on the tempting slack in his lower lip as he tried to stop her or the way the warmth from his hand was sending shockwaves through her.

"Champagne is for celebrating. I'd rather save it for later."

Astrid waited for a heartbeat or two, then plunged the bottle back into the ice bucket. "Fine." She would not let this development ruin her evening. *Later* sounded vaguely promising. She'd cling to whatever hope she could.

Five

Clay didn't like to worry. It was a waste of time and energy, especially when he found himself doing it over things he couldn't control, like the Architect of the Year awards. "You can't do a thing about it. Relax," he said to himself in the mirror as he straightened his bowtie.

But I care about this. Thus he was stuck in what felt like an endless cycle of unease. As much as he didn't care about other people's opinions, and was confident in his work, there was this part of him that needed the validation of the award. With little to no parental guidance as a kid, he'd spent his entire life without a stamp of approval from anyone, except perhaps Miranda. Their grandmother certainly hadn't provided it. If anything, she'd treated the two of them as a burden. He wanted this accolade. He'd worked so hard to get it.

He took a cleansing breath, determined to shake off his unsettled feelings. He just needed to get through the next few hours until they announced the winner. Then he'd deal with whatever had happened. And for now, perhaps it was best to focus on his next challenge: facing Astrid and whatever maddening dress she'd chosen for tonight.

He opened the door to his room and strode out into the central living area of their suite. He wasn't the type to pace, but he found himself doing exactly that, thinking about Astrid in her room...wondering what state of dress, or undress, she might be in. He swallowed hard, realizing what an additional test this would be, spending the evening with Astrid when he was admittedly already weak. It was creating a whole new layer of trepidation within him, one that he felt physically. Yes, she was there for moral support. Nothing else. But if he was being honest, he wanted more.

For the time being, he needed a drink to soothe his ragged edges. He should have taken Astrid's suggestion that they open the champagne an hour ago, but he hadn't. He'd made the excuse that it was for celebrating, when in reality he saw it as too romantic. Now, he could easily imagine the repercussions of opening it without her. She'd be mad. So instead, he went for a bottle of good bourbon from the well-stocked bar. Clay unscrewed the top and poured a healthy dose into a cut crystal glass. It was nearly to his lips when he heard Astrid's door open behind him. He turned, and the instant he saw her, the only logical reaction was to toss back his drink. The whole thing. One gulp.

"Thirsty?" Astrid asked.

He nodded eagerly, unable to peel his eyes from the vision of her. She was nothing short of pure elegance in a deep blue dress that showed off her beauty in a way that nothing she'd ever worn to work could possibly do. The gown clung to her upper arms, flaunting her sculpted shoulders and dewy skin. The neckline was understated, but dipped low enough to drive him crazy, accentuating the swell of her bust. It took too little effort for his mind to sketch in the hidden details of her breasts, the fullness and what they might feel like in his hands. Her long and graceful neck was adorned with a single gleaming gem in a square cut hanging from a chain.

"Is that a diamond?" he asked, fighting for his voice to reach full volume.

Her slender fingers found the stone. Something about seeing her touch herself made the tension in his hips grow even tighter. "It is. It was a gift from Johnathon. I couldn't bear to part with it, even after the divorce."

There was the reminder of just how intertwined Clay and Astrid were—she and his sister had been married to the same man. Astrid owned a chunk of the company he worked for. There were a million reasons to not feel the way he did about her, but there seemed to be just as many thinly veiled excuses to pick her up and take her back into the bedroom right now. His dream might be waiting downstairs in the hotel ballroom, but it also felt like it was standing right in front of him.

Get your head on straight.

"It's beautiful." He poured himself another drink and downed it just as fast. The burn was vicious, and he knew that he deserved it for the things that were going through his head right now. "Can I make you a drink? Or we could open the champagne if you really want to."

"I'll take one of whatever you're having." She floated closer to him, bringing along his first real breath of her perfume. It was warm and sweet, just like her. "You were right. We should save the champagne for after the ceremony. To celebrate your achievement."

"Stop saying that."

She took one more step, closing the gap between them. She smoothed the lapel of his jacket, while all he could do was stare down at her hand on his chest and fight the wish that he wasn't wearing this suit and her dress was puddled on the floor. "I believe in the power of positive thinking. You're brilliant and talented. The rest will work itself out."

It was a mystery how she could have so much confidence in him when she'd only known him for a few months. He'd had to live with himself for thirty-five years and he wasn't convinced of anything she was saying. "But the decision has already been made. Somewhere downstairs in the hotel ballroom is an envelope with a name on it that might not be mine."

She peered up at him, her impossibly warm eyes flickering with optimism. "Positive thinking, Clay. Only good thoughts." She patted his chest, then looked away. "Now, where's my drink?"

"Oh. Right." Clay felt as though half of his brain had suddenly decided to take the night off. He grabbed a second glass and poured a splash of bourbon for her.

Meanwhile, Astrid traipsed over to the end table next to one of the sofas and picked up the house phone. "Yes. Hello. We have a bottle of champagne in our room that needs fresh ice." She grinned at him, her whole face lighting up with a hint of mischief. "We're going to be celebrating later this evening and it would be a shame if it had gone warm."

He was so drawn to her right now, it was comical. If only she knew she could ask him for anything and he would give it to her without reservation. "Thank you for doing that," he said as she ended the call. "I'm sorry I didn't want to open the bottle earlier."

"I understand you're feeling superstitious. It's okay."

Once again, Astrid saw right through him. "It sounds silly, though, doesn't it? Plus, you're the one who's talking about being positive. I'm not employing logic or optimism."

"You really are worked up about tonight, aren't you? All that talk about nerves was real."

"I'm sure it makes me seem like a fool, but yes. I don't enjoy crowds. I don't enjoy phony social situations, and I do not relish the thought of sitting in that room, hearing my name announced among the nominees, and not ultimately hearing that I won. I know it won't be the end of the world, but I'm still dreading that moment."

She approached him slowly, making him feel like he was a buck alone in a meadow, poised to run off into the woods at any time. Stopping mere inches from him, she reached up and reassuringly rubbed his arm, and his defenses wavered. It would be so simple to kiss her and take her in his arms.

"I think you need to give up control tonight," she said in a calm and measured tone.

"Excuse me?"

"You like to be in charge. You like to manage every little thing. But it's not going to work in this situation. You have no control."

"So what do I do? Radically change my personality and suddenly become laid back and relaxed?"

She shook her head. "No. You put me in the driver's seat. I am in charge. You do what I say. No exceptions."

He didn't mean to scoff at her suggestion, but the breathy grunt escaped his lips before he could even think about it. "That won't work."

"But it will. I just need you to trust me."

"I don't do that, either."

She fluttered her long, dark lashes at him—it felt deeply manipulative and yet it might have been the sexiest thing he'd seen in his lifetime. "Let me put it this way. If you don't give me control, I'm leaving. Do you want me to go?"

He tried not to look at the enticing contours of her bare collarbone or think about what it might be like to kiss her there, but he failed. The thought of Astrid abandoning him was unthinkable, even for the man who'd spent so much time pushing her away. "No. I don't want you to go."

Astrid wasn't about to gloat over her win in getting Clay to acquiesce to her plan. At least not outwardly. On the inside, she was doing a victory dance. Progress. Finally. If nothing else good happened in the next twenty-four hours, she would at least know that she'd convinced him of something.

She held his hand on the elevator as they rode down to the lobby. He shot her a questioning look when she first did it, and she returned the expression, but hers came with two arched eyebrows and the subliminal reminder that she was in charge and he'd better not question her methods. Luckily, the presence of several other guests kept him quiet. She knew that human contact would help him stay grounded. It would help him relax. Even when he radiated so much tension she was worried he might snap in two.

Downstairs, they wound their way through the

elegant lobby and back to the ballroom where the
dinner and awards ceremony were being held. They
waited in line to check in, and Astrid noticed that
there was a photographer with professional lighting
and a backdrop waiting for them after that step. She
already anticipated that Clay wouldn't want his picture taken, and she armed herself with the appropriate argument.

"Yes. Hi. Astrid Sterling and Clay Morgan," he
said when they reached the table. "We're both with
Sterling Enterprises in San Diego."

Astrid hadn't realized how much pride she would
take in her job and the fact that she worked with Clay
until she heard him say that. It made her heart swell.

"Yes, Mr. Morgan. We have you at table two right
in front of the stage. Good luck this evening."

"Just what I wanted," Clay muttered sarcastically
to Astrid. "To be on full display, right in the very
front of the room."

"Optimism. Think of it as a shorter walk if you
win." She nodded at the photographer. "Ready to
get your picture taken, guy who doesn't want to be
in the spotlight?"

"Do we have to?"

"Yes. We do. You'll be fine. I've done this a million times."

"Am I supposed to stand a certain way?"

"One hand in your pants pocket, the other at your
side. Don't square your shoulders to the camera." She
tugged on his hand until they were standing before

the backdrop. Astrid instinctively angled her body and placed her hand on her hip.

Clay took her directions perfectly. So much so that the photographer took note. "You two look like you've done this before."

Clay actually smiled. "It's all her. She's the pro."

"Well, you look amazing together. Enjoy your night."

Astrid could hardly contain her grin as they strolled into the room. She was certain that they *did* look good together. Very, very good. "Shall we get a drink before they have us sit for dinner?"

"Yes. Let's see if there's anyone you need to meet."

Astrid relinquished a bit of control as she allowed Clay to lead the way through the throng of people in the ballroom. A steady din of conversation fought with the jazz piped through the sound system, and Astrid couldn't help but notice that there weren't nearly enough women in the room. She worked in what was still a male-dominated industry, which only made her want to recommit herself to her role at Sterling. She, Tara, and Miranda were in a position of power and they couldn't squander the opportunity.

"What would you like to drink?" Clay asked.

Of course he didn't know her cocktail of choice— this was one of very few times they'd seen each other in a social setting. "White wine."

"Nothing stronger?"

"I need to keep my wits about me. I am in charge

tonight." Again, he smiled, fueling Astrid's desire for him. *Focus on the awards. Focus on support.*

After Clay got their drinks from the bar, he spotted a few people he wanted her to meet, mostly architects from the firm in Santa Barbara where he'd once worked. "I want you all to meet Astrid Sterling. Astrid and I work together. She's the project manager for our bid on the Seaport Promenade project in San Diego."

"I hear good things," one of the men said. "The buzz is that Sterling is at the top of the heap for that one."

"We still have two more phases of the bid process to go through until it's final," Astrid said. "But thank you. I appreciate your kind words."

"Astrid is amazing," Clay said. "She's so good at keeping us on schedule that we're actually a bit ahead of the game."

Astrid could've been knocked over by a puff of air. Clay spent so much time saying they didn't work well together. It never occurred to her that he actually thought she did a good job. Of course, she wasn't about to let on while they were standing with a group of their peers, but she did tuck away the compliment in her memory. She'd keep it close for quite some time. "Clay's the real rock star of our team," Astrid said. "Without him, we wouldn't stand a chance."

"Exactly why he was nominated tonight," the man said, just as a chime was sounded, announcing that everyone should take their seats for dinner. "Wishing you the best of luck."

Astrid and Clay found their seats at table two, where it turned out they were seated with the other three finalists and their guests. After cursory introductions, Clay sat next to Astrid, his face drawn with stress. "This is all too real."

"Real is good," she whispered into his ear, letting her mouth linger near his neck so she could breathe in the warm scent of his cologne.

He reached under the table and took her hand, making her heart nearly stop beating. His mouth was right by her cheek, his breath soft against her skin. "Whatever happens tonight, I'm glad you're here."

"I wouldn't want to be anywhere else."

Dinner was soon served—a succulent red snapper with Thai flavors of coconut milk, lemongrass, and ginger, along with jasmine rice and sautéed spinach. Clay picked through his plate, not seeming interested in food.

"Don't you like it?" Astrid asked.

"It's delicious. I just don't have an appetite."

Astrid hated seeing him like this. She wished she could push fast-forward on the ceremony so he could get on with his life. "Does that mean I can have your dessert?"

Clay slung his arm over the back of Astrid's chair, which made her sit a little straighter in her seat. It made her dig deep for breaths. "If there's chocolate, probably not."

"Fair enough."

The dessert did indeed have chocolate—a flourless cake with a salted caramel drizzle. Everyone was enjoying it, even Clay, when a woman took the stage and began the presentation. Again, Clay set aside his fork, seeming disinterested. *It really must be bad if he isn't finishing that cake.* She was beginning to see that he had a weakness for sweets.

He shifted in his seat as the first slate of awards were given, all in the area of residential architecture, which was not Clay's area of expertise. The plates were cleared from the tables, glasses of champagne were delivered to all, and Clay continued to struggle to sit still. Astrid would have done anything to make his trepidation go away. As the awards shifted to commercial architecture, she leaned closer and raised her head to speak into his ear. "You're almost there. Just breathe."

He nodded, looking down at the table and a cocktail napkin that he was folding and unfolding with one hand, like he was creating the origami equivalent of worry beads. Astrid decided she would occupy his other hand, so she reached under the table and found it resting on his firm and muscular thigh. She pushed past her own desire to explore his long limbs and instead squeezed his hand. Every time he cleared his throat or shifted in his seat, she held it tight again.

"And finally, we come to the final award of the night. The Architect of the Year. As you all know, this award is open to both commercial and residential architects, so it really does represent the best of the best in our state. The nominees have demonstrated excellence with their vision, creativity, professionalism, and devotion to their craft."

The room was remarkably quiet and Astrid found herself now being as nervous as Clay was. Possibly more so. What was going to happen if he didn't win? Why had she been so stupid as to assure him that he would? She could easily imagine what their working relationship was going to become if he did end up losing. She would be an everyday reminder of the milestone he hadn't reached. It had her rethinking every optimistic thing she'd said over the last few hours. So much for her ridiculous attraction to him. She might have ruined any chance she ever had.

The show host announced the nominees, but the names came out muffled as Astrid's mind swirled with worry.

And then, just like that, it cleared.

"The winner is Clay Morgan, Sterling Enterprises."

Astrid and Clay looked at each other and froze. Then they both burst out laughing. Before she could think how to act, she found herself bolting up out of her seat and wrapping him up in the most enthusiastic hug she'd ever given anyone.

"Thank you," he said, loud and clear and right to her, as the audience rose to their feet and erupted in applause.

"Get up there," Astrid blurted. "You can thank me later."

Clay ascended the stairs up onto the stage and accepted his award. The way he admired the figurine told Astrid all she needed to know. The expression on his face was one of pure satisfaction and pride. "Wow," Clay said into the microphone. "Thank you for this honor. It means so much to me. I won't bore you with a long speech, but I want to thank everyone at Sterling Enterprises. Our team is incredible. I also want to thank my sister and my daughter, neither of whom could be here tonight, but to whom I owe everything. They are my life." He drew a deep breath and a pleased smile bloomed on his face. "Thank you."

Astrid was exactly the sort of woman to cry at happy moments, and the tears were streaming down her cheeks as she watched Clay leave the stage and accept congratulations from the people he passed on his way back to their table.

When he reached her, he was shaking his head. "I should have thanked you specifically from the stage. I'm so sorry. My mind was a blur up there."

"But you did thank me. I'm part of the team." She waved it off, not wanting to admit that she was slightly disappointed to not have her name mentioned. "Don't worry about it. I'm just happy for you."

"But you are an important part of my work life

and I've been a jerk. I guess it took spending this time with you to see that we *can* work well together."

Astrid was flushed with warmth from head to toe. She was not only immensely proud of him for his award, she was glad they'd finally broken through a barrier together. Was this a taste of things to come? Could he ever let her in? "I'm so happy to hear that."

"Not half as happy as I am, knowing that you and I have a bottle of champagne waiting for us upstairs."

Six

"You're sure you don't want to go to the reception?" Astrid had been struggling to get a word in. A constant stream of friends, acquaintances, and even strangers kept stopping to congratulate Clay as they filed out of the ballroom. "I'm sure the other winners will all be there."

"Going to a party is the last thing I want to do." It wasn't the celebration of the award that he'd been seeking. It was the recognition. As far as he was concerned, that could have been a quiet exercise. It didn't have to be a big show. But there was more to his disinterest in the party than that. Here in a different town, away from the office, his family and outside influences, Astrid was the center of his orbit right now. She had made this night amazing. She'd forced him out of his own head and out of his comfort zone. If he'd been left to his own devices, he would have been his usual one-man island. And he didn't have to imagine the empty feeling he would've been stuck with if he'd been here all alone. He knew that feeling all too well.

"So we'll go upstairs and toast your big win?"

"As long as you're okay with it. I don't want you to miss out on any fun. You look so beautiful in that dress. I wouldn't blame you if you wanted to make the rounds at the party."

"Are you flirting with me, Clay?"

It was no longer an easy task to breathe. *One kiss. That's all I need.* But he would not kiss her. He wasn't even sure she was attracted to him. Still, he was prepared to be honest with her about his reasons for having struggled to work with her. She deserved the truth. She'd earned it. He was prepared to live with the consequences.

"It's not flirtation. It's the truth." The ballroom had largely emptied out. "You are easily the most beautiful woman I have ever seen. I'm sure hundreds of men have told you that."

Her eyes bore no judgment for what he'd admitted. Only curiosity. "You really think that?"

"Isn't it a bit obvious?"

"Hundreds of men have not told me that. Not the way you did just now, with sincerity."

"You must have left a long string of broken hearts behind you."

She shook her head slowly, never breaking eye contact with him. "No. I haven't. Men will admire me, but they don't have the nerve to be honest with me in any real way."

"That's important to you? Honesty?"

"Immensely."

This was as good a time as any to come clean. "If we're being honest, Astrid, I need to tell you that I have struggled with being very attracted to you." He watched as her eyes flickered with a mix of surprise and delight. He wasn't about to wait for her response. "But I want you to know that it's not just because you're stunning. You're so open and generous. You're so sweet. I don't really know what to make of it. I only know that I'm drawn to you."

She cracked half a smile and shied away for a split second. "You wouldn't say I'm so sweet if you knew what I was thinking about you in that suit."

Clay's sights narrowed on her, but he caught the corners of his mouth trying to twitch into a smile. "What?"

"You're not the only one who's struggled with attraction, Clay. My jaw dropped the first time I met you."

Ripples of heat began moving through him, like a tide that rolled in but never receded. "Wow. I was not expecting you to say that."

"Did I manage to surprise the unflappable Clay

Morgan?" Her eyes glinted with flirtation, sending his brain off in a very specific direction, the one that led them upstairs.

"You did. And the only thing that will help me shake off my surprise is a glass of champagne. In our room."

"Exactly what I was thinking." Astrid hooked her arm in his and they beelined for the door.

Outside the ballroom, there were dozens of people still milling about and talking. Clay ducked through the crowd, pulling Astrid behind him in his wake. When they broke free, it was her turn to tug on him as she took extra long strides across the lobby—so long that Clay noticed something he hadn't before. Her gown had a high slit. That flash of her bare skin spiked his body temperature so much he nearly broke out in a sweat.

Luckily, the elevator had just dropped off a handful of guests when they reached it. They hopped on board and Clay jabbed the button for the top floor of the hotel, then went for the one that would close the doors. They were both short of breath after rushing through the lobby, and Clay couldn't help but have his sights drawn to Astrid's décolletage as every inhalation filled out her curves. She was a feast for the senses, without so much as a single touch.

They were about to reach their floor when Astrid dropped her clutch handbag. Clay bent down to pick it up just as Astrid did the same, except she crouched, which caused her leg to poke out through the slit, all the way to her very upper thigh. The elevator dinged and the door slid open, but they were both frozen, staring at each other. It felt like a silent admission that something was going to happen between them. He hoped like hell neither of them lived to regret crossing that line.

They stepped out into the hall and the sense of urgency between them was even more pronounced than it had been downstairs. Clay pulled loose his bow tie as he strode ahead. He couldn't take it anymore. Something had started downstairs and continued in the elevator. Hell, it started the minute they met. But he'd had enough of resisting her appeal. Spending every minute with her in the office and all day on their trip together had been too great a test.

Every inch of Astrid was temptation. Next to her in the elevator, the view had been incredible, but looking was no longer enough. He needed to touch her, without that beautiful dress. He wanted her in his bed, so he could get lost in her, if only for one night. This was their chance and he sensed it. Back in San Diego, everything and everyone else would get in the way.

He flashed his key in front of the electronic sensor and the lock clicked open. Holding the door for her, he filled his lungs with the soft strains of her perfume. He didn't know what would happen next and he would follow her lead, but his heart was still thumping out a steadfast beat, like his own body was trying to remind him to take note of what might be about to happen.

He closed the door behind them as Astrid placed her bag on the table in the entry. She planted her hand against the wall and kicked off her shoes. "These things are killing me."

Clay laughed quietly. Her former career had been built on fashion, but she wasn't afraid to be real with him. He stooped down to pick them up for her and that was when she placed her hand on his shoulder. On bended knee, he gazed up at her. It was the perfect illustration of the way he viewed their dynamic—he was at her mercy and in perpetual awe. "I was trying to be a gentleman."

She nodded slowly, and it felt like seduction, the way her face was beckoning him. "I know you were. And I adore you for it." Her other hand went to the side of his face, her palm pressed against his cheek. "I like you, Clay. I like you a lot. Even when you don't always seem to like me…"

He placed his hand on his knee and pushed himself to standing. "No. Stop." He took one of her hands. "I have always liked you. I just haven't always liked the way I am around you. That's my fault. Not yours."

"I know you like control. Does it maybe feel like you lose it when you're around me?"

"That's probably part of it. I don't like knowing that I have any weaknesses at all."

"We all do. It's part of being human."

If only she understood that her reasoning brought him no comfort. "We need to stop talking about me. I want to know what you want." He rubbed the back of her hand with his thumb.

"Are we talking about right this minute, or long-term?" She cocked one of her perfectly groomed eyebrows at him.

Any discussion of the future would only circle back to his cache of reasons to avoid anything physical or romantic with Astrid. "I vote for right this minute."

She popped up onto her tiptoes and reached for his neck. "I want this." Before he could think twice about what she was doing, her lips were on his, just as soft and giving as everything else about Astrid. *Is this happening?* Her mouth was so lush, it took his breath away. Wanting to be closer to her, he lowered his head, and she responded by running her tongue along his lower lip and punctuating it with the gentlest of nips. *Wow.* He tightened his arms around her waist, tugging her closer as she bowed into him, doing everything he could to not rove too far with his hands. He wanted nothing more than to bunch the supple fabric of her dress in his hands, walk his fingers through it until he reached stretches of her skin. Just the thought of touching her like that made his body go tight. He wanted her in ways he couldn't begin to understand. These weeks of admiring her every day, wanting and resisting, had forced his mind and body into a war—this first glimmer of a truce was so heavenly he would have waved one hundred flags of surrender.

"I need to know that this is really what you want, Astrid," he said. His mouth wandered to her jaw and then her neck, his lips skimming the chain that held the diamond pendant at her throat. The kisses were meant to put this all on pause for a few seconds while she answered, but she let out a soft moan of appreciation that felt like her attempt to pour gasoline on the flame. "If even one inch of that dress comes off, if we have sex, our entire dynamic at work is going to change."

She reared back her head and narrowed her gaze. "Are you kidding me? I want to destroy the way we interact at work." She threaded her hands inside his jacket, rolling them over his shoulders until she could push the garment to the floor. "I want to set it on fire and let it burn until it's a pile of ashes."

He'd never heard such colorful consent. Damn, he was a lucky man. And not because he'd won a major award earlier that evening. "Okay, then. Let's melt it to the ground."

Astrid's mind was like a tornado in the heat of summer, a whorl of thoughts at conflict with each other, fueled by the electricity that sparked out of thin air. She wanted him so badly it hurt to think about it, but she had no earthly idea what was on the other side of making love to Clay. Would this change their working relationship for the better? Was she really lucky enough to have that happen?

She reminded herself that even if she had answers to her questions, there were no guarantees, especially with a man as hard to pin down as Clay. Better to give in to what she wanted and actually pin him down—to her bed. Now that his jacket was gone, she went for his shirt, untucking it, then letting her fingers race through the buttons. He kissed her neck again and she reached back to unlatch her necklace, placing it on the table. His mouth was unbelievable and that hit of wet heat against her skin made a real task of keeping her eyes open. She just wanted to let them drift shut, so she could give in to his ministrations. But now that his shirt was on the floor, she had to admire the firm plane of his chest.

She flattened her hands against his hard pecs and kissed her way across the broad expanse. His hands went to the zipper of her dress, drawing it down slowly, a hint of cooler air hitting her skin as he went. The sleeves slumped to her elbows, but the tight-fitting bodice still covered her breasts. She wanted nothing more than to be bare to him. Vulnerable. So she took a single step back and straightened her arms, letting the weight of the gown pull it down past her chest, waist, and legs, giving him full view of her in only a lacy black strapless bra and matching panties.

Clay's eyes went even darker as they raked over her body, his expression full of hunger. "I know I keep saying this, but you are unbelievably beautiful." He cradled her face with both hands, bringing her lips to his, then turned her around until her back was to him. He unhooked her bra, then pulled her shoulders back against his chest. He placed his hands flat against her lower belly, his fingertips brushing the top edge of her panties, then caressed his way up until the hands she had admired countless times were cupping her breasts. Her nipples went hard from his warm touch. Her spine tingled. He took full advantage, rolling the tight buds of sensitive skin between his thumbs and index fingers. It was as if he'd closed a circuit in her body, sending zaps of electricity down her stomach and between her legs. She needed his touch there. She craved it. The longing was so fierce that she whimpered.

She took his hands and pulled them down her stomach, hoping to convey her wants. He took the hint and nudged her panties down past her hips. Astrid wriggled out of them, feeling deliciously free. It wasn't an equitable situation, though, so she went straight for his pants, unbuttoning, unzipping, and tugging them and his boxers out of the way. She didn't want to stare, but he was magnificent now that she could see all of him…every last inch. She kissed him softly, reaching down and taking his erection in her hand. He groaned from that first touch, a sound that dipped lower as she took long, careful strokes. He got harder in her hand, further showing his approval by deepening their kiss. She could feel the old walls between them melting away. She couldn't have guessed how good it would feel.

Clay took her hand and led her to one of the plush upholstered chairs. He pressed lightly on her shoulder and she sat, not knowing what he was doing or what he wanted. The anticipation was killing her, but every tick of the clock brought another gleeful discovery, a glimpse into what Clay Morgan wanted. What he liked. Astrid took note of it all, hoping that she might get a chance to use this knowledge more than once.

He dropped to his knees, his eyes full of a fiery lust. It was such a turn-on to take in the visible evidence of his desire. He took one of her calves and draped it over his shoulder, spreading her legs wide and urging her to lean back in the chair. He kissed her belly, then the inside of her thigh, blazing a trail with his mouth straight to her center.

Astrid gasped when his mouth found her apex and he rolled his tongue in tight circles. Her eyes clamped shut, her hands raking deep into his thick hair and curling into his scalp. He slid a finger inside her, then two, satisfying yet another desire as he curled into her most sensitive spot. The pressure built quickly. Higher and higher, then another step closer again. Her breaths were hard and short as she teetered on the brink. Then he sent her sailing past her peak, right over the edge. She arched her back and gave in to the jolt of pleasure, and the waves that followed, all while he pressed his unbelievable lips to the sensitive inside of her thighs. As her mind slipped into the present, she knew one thing: she wanted him inside her.

She sat up and kissed him. "Do you have a condom? Please tell me you do."

He frowned. "Maybe in my toiletry kit. I'm not sure."

Astrid did not have one. She hadn't been intimately involved with a man in three years. There'd been no one since Johnathon. It all made sense, but now that she was thinking about it, she did wonder why she'd allowed herself to be so unprepared. She really had been reluctant to admit how much she wanted Clay. "We have to look. I need you."

They both hurried to their feet and rushed into his bedroom, then into his bathroom. Clay dug through the bag as Astrid stood behind him and kissed his back, her hands on his hips. "One," he announced. "I found one."

"Perfect. That's good enough." She plucked it from his hand, ready to take charge. She wanted to rock his world. She wanted to show him that they could work together perfectly. No, this wasn't the office, but there were other ways to demonstrate compatibility.

She grabbed his hand and walked backward into his bedroom, pulling him along as she went. He grinned like a man who knew he was in for something good. *You have no idea.* She stretched out on the silky bedding and he did the same, their bodies drawn together as lips met lips, arms coiled around the other, and Astrid hitched her leg around Clay's hip. His fingers dug into the fleshiest parts of her bottom, telling her how badly he wanted her. The feeling was mutual.

Astrid pushed him to his back and kneeled between his legs. She drew a finger up the center of his thigh, from his knee to the deep contour along his hip. He closed his eyes and rolled his head to one side as she repeated the trail on the other side.

"Do you want me to touch you?" she asked. The answer was obvious, but she still wanted to hear it.

"Yes. Please."

She lowered her head and huffed warm air against his length. "What about now?"

"Now you're just being mean," he groaned. "Although I like it. I like you being mean."

She planted her hands on either side of his chest and kissed his pecs softly, all while her thigh brushed against his erection. "I don't have it in me to be cruel. I just want to make you happy." She didn't want to make him beg. That wasn't her point. She only wanted it to be amazing. She reached down and took him in her hand, wrapping her fingers around him tightly.

"I'm happy as long as you're touching me."

She smiled to herself, caressing his length, up, rolling her palm over the tip, down to the base, tightening her grip as she went. Again, she made mental notes of his reactions, the things that made his mouth go slack with pleasure. She also loved having this small bit of control over him. Normally she felt as though she was at such a disadvantage.

He popped up to his elbows and opened his eyes. "I can't wait any more. I need to be inside you." He took one hand and pushed her hair from her face tenderly and kissed her—a slow, soft, wet kiss.

"I want you, too, Clay." Funny how there were no negotiations inside the bedroom. Only agreement. She took the condom from the bedside table and opened the pouch, rolling it onto him carefully.

He watched every move she made, not tearing his sights from her. The instant she was done, he pulled her down on top of him, then rolled her to her back. It was so forceful and strong, it nearly knocked the breath out of her. She hadn't felt that desired and wanted for so long. There at his mercy, she dropped her knees, opening herself to him. The wall was about to be gone.

He drove inside, and she waited for the moment when she would slip into the haze of pleasure and the world around her would recede. But that didn't happen with Clay. As much as she'd dreamed of this, he made it very, very real. He delivered the strokes so artfully that there was no choice but to pay attention. To meet every motion he made with a rock of her hips, and every kiss with one of her own.

He placed a hand on one side of her face, holding up his body weight with his other arm. "Talk to me, Astrid. Tell me what you need."

For that man of few words, this was a surprise

indeed. "Now you want me to talk?" she kidded, raising her head and kissing his chest, then his neck.

"This is important. I don't want you to be anything less than satisfied."

The truth was that this had already far surpassed her hopes, but she shifted herself a tiny bit, then grasped his shoulder, pulling him down. "I need your body weight on me."

"I'll crush you."

"You won't."

She pulled her knees higher, enjoying every incredible inch of him as he rode inside and out. "That's it. Right there."

He sank down against her, adding to the pressure, kissing her deeply and with unending passion. She explored his back, found his incredible ass, giving him a good grab. All the while, each thrust brought her closer to the edge. Her insides were tightening, coiling and about to spring at any second.

"I'm close," she muttered. Her peak was toying with her, pushing closer, then pulling away.

"Me, too. You feel so amazing."

She smiled and nestled her face in his neck, letting his stubble rub against her cheeks. She closed her eyes, her muscles contracting faster. He matched her intensity and she clutched his body, grabbing him with everything inside her. She called out sharply as the pleasure drove through her. Then Clay followed, his torso going rigid for a moment, then relaxing as he gave in to it all. He collapsed at her side, but immediately pulled her close, into the safe and warm cocoon of his arms. She hadn't expected post-sex snuggling. Not from Clay. This was so much like an expression of affection.

He was a man of many surprises. No question about that. "That was incredible." She sighed, drinking in his smell and still not quite believing this had happened. She'd fantasized about it so many times, but to her great surprise, her mind hadn't managed to make it anywhere close to this good.

Seven

Clay woke with a hum of satisfaction in his body and the pleasing warmth of Astrid's even breaths on his chest. Her head rested on his shoulder, silky hair draped on his arm, a delicate hand on his stomach, and long leg wrapped around his. He was blissfully aware of the press of her soft breasts against his rib cage, and of the velvety contours of her lower back as he settled his own hand there. It had been a long time since he'd experienced this much closeness with a woman, and he was a man divided against himself because of it. The sunnier parts of him could get used to this. But his more pragmatic side was fighting against that, telling him to run. It was an insidious loop to be stuck in. His past had worn a rut in his thinking, but there was certainty in remaining romantically unattached. There was safety there. For himself, but more importantly, for his daughter.

Still, Astrid was simply amazing. Last night had been electrifying, their physical connection intense. He wanted more of what they'd shared, but that was the irrational part of his brain whispering that it would be okay to wade back into these waters. The truth was that he couldn't put life on pause. They were about to drive back to San Diego in a few hours. He would spend his weekend with Delia. He and Astrid would return to work on Monday. And they had just managed to make their professional relationship even more complicated. He'd made a mistake, and now he had to fix it.

He was mulling over how to address this with Astrid when his phone rang. He glanced at the clock on the bedside table. It was nine a.m. This was likely Miranda and Delia.

"Astrid. I need to get this call." He uncoiled himself from her and scrambled across the room for his phone. To make matters worse, it was a video call. He pressed Accept, but left the phone facing up, so the only view Delia and Miranda would get would be of the ceiling. "Hey, guys. What's up?" He quickly put on his boxers, then grabbed the jeans he'd packed from his suitcase.

"Why are we looking at a ceiling?" Miranda asked.

Across the room, Astrid was sitting up in bed,

pushing her messy hair back from her face. How was she so damn beautiful, even first thing in the morning?

"Sorry," Clay said. "I'm putting on a shirt. I just got out of bed." He held a finger to his lips to silently beg Astrid to be quiet.

"We called to say congratulations," Miranda said. "We were surprised you didn't call us last night, but Tara texted me to say she was excited that you won."

Guilt washed over him. He'd reached his pinnacle and hadn't thought to call the two most important people in the world. Now that he was dressed, he picked up his phone and looked at the screen. There were Delia and Miranda, sitting on the sofa in her living room. "I'm so sorry. There was a big party afterward and so many people. I just didn't have a spare minute to myself." He hated that little white lie. He had totally fallen down on the job by not calling them last night. This was the perfect illustration of how much he allowed himself to be distracted by Astrid. He lost all coherent thought when he was with her.

"Party?" Miranda asked, seeming incredulous. "You hate parties."

"You do hate parties," Astrid whispered to him as she climbed out of bed. "Don't lie about it."

Clay shushed her.

"Did you just shush me?" Miranda asked.

"I don't always hate them," Clay shot back as Astrid walked up to him, completely naked. Her body was so incredible it made his head swim—her rounded hips, her lovely breasts, and her lush bottom. She was a feast for the senses. He was not sated. And he had to get over it.

"Daddy, when are you coming home?" Delia asked.

Clay glanced at Astrid as she walked away from him to the bathroom, wagging her hips with every step. *Never? Is that a valid answer?* "Soon, honey. Soon. I need to shower and pack up and grab some breakfast. I should be back a little after lunchtime."

"So Aunt Miranda and I can go swimming?"

"Take your time," Miranda said with a quick arch of her eyebrows. Was she on to him? He never should have asked for advice about Astrid. He never should have put the thought in his sister's head. He'd hoped she could help him straighten out his thinking, but she'd had to go and muddy the waters with that stuff about staying open to the idea of love. That was an easier prospect for Miranda. She'd lost the person she loved by a cruel twist of fate. He'd had to find out that he'd married and had a child with someone he'd read all wrong. That mistake would always hang over his head.

"Love you both," he said.

"Love you, too," Miranda and Delia said in response.

Clay ended the call, his heart and conscience heavy.

He looked up to see Astrid standing in the doorway to the bathroom, leaning against the frame, her glorious body on full display. "Did I hear something about a shower?" She punctuated the question with a subtle pout.

He knew that what he was about to say would come out badly, but he also didn't want to lead Astrid down a path where he wasn't clear about his intentions. She deserved better than that. He wasn't about to be the man who took what he wanted and then ended it all. It wouldn't be right to do so.

He rose from his chair and approached her. With every step closer, his stomach knotted tighter and he regretted his situation a little more. She was so tempting. She was quite possibly the perfect woman. But she was also an unknown quantity. They barely knew each other. That made her dangerous. It was one thing to put his heart on the line, but he wouldn't do that to Delia. "I do need to take a shower, but I wanted to talk first."

She wrapped her arms around his neck, digging her fingers into his nape. Her nakedness was so distracting—every part of her that he wanted to touch was mere inches away. "What do you want to talk about?" She popped up onto her tiptoes and kissed his neck.

His hands reflexively went to her hips, and the instant his skin touched hers, the battle inside his body was reborn. His need for her was fiery and intense, making every drop of blood race to the center of his body. He wanted her so badly he couldn't see straight. "Us. Last night."

"It was amazing," she whispered into his ear.

"It was. It absolutely was. But we didn't talk about our personal situations before clothes started to come off, and getting that call from Miranda and Delia just now only reminded me that I have other people to worry about other than myself."

"Oh. Okay." She dropped back down to her flat feet and stepped back from him. "I guess we could talk about it now."

"My situation is complicated. Which is why I fought my attraction to you. I can't get involved with someone. It's not that easy. I need to focus on Delia's happiness. She's been through so much."

Astrid walked over to the vanity and grabbed a towel, wrapping it around her body. "Of course. I understand."

But did she? Really? She didn't know the harsh truths of his past, and he intended it to stay that way. "And then there's work. You and I both know what the rumor mill is like in that office. If anyone gets wind of this, it'll be all anyone talks about. You have a financial stake in the company and so does my sister. Can you see how this isn't a great idea?"

Astrid's face fell, but she very quickly forced a smile on her face. "Don't take everything so seriously, Clay. This was just a little sex between friends. No big deal."

"Are you sure?" Nothing in her expression matched her words.

"Yes. You worry too much. I've told you that before." She patted him on the shoulder. "I'll take a shower in my own bathroom."

Clay swallowed hard, realizing what he had just passed up. *I'm either super smart or a complete idiot.* "Ready to go in an hour?"

"I can do that." She nodded and started for the door.

"Do you want me to call down to room service and order coffee? Maybe some pastries?" He was so pathetic, trying to ply her with sweets.

"It's okay. I'm not hungry." With that, she disappeared.

Clay sighed and walked into his bathroom, planting both hands on the vanity and staring at his own reflection. How had everything gone so upside down? Last night, he'd been on top of the world. And that wasn't merely because of the award. Astrid had made him feel alive in ways he hadn't experienced in a very long time.

But his needs and wants weren't what was most important. This was a question of priorities. He and Astrid had work to accomplish together. And Clay had a daughter and his heart to protect.

As soon as Astrid stepped out of Clay's bedroom, she was confronted by too many reminders of last night. The champagne in the bucket, still not consumed and probably room temperature by now. Her diamond pendant on the table, the one that Johnathon had given her so many years ago. And last, there was

Clay's tux and her dress, intermingled on the floor. She might have had the time of her life last night, but now it was the next, very depressing day.

She gathered the necklace, her gown and her undies from the floor and carried them into her room, tossing them onto the still-made bed. She was angry, frustrated and confused, but she was not going to allow her hopes to be crushed by a man. She'd been through that routine hundreds of times during her marriage to Johnathon. It might be a well-worn path, but she was damned if she was going to get back on it. It didn't matter that the man putting her on notice was Clay, and that she'd wanted him from the moment she'd met him. She'd had her taste and now he was taking that away. It was his choice. Now she needed to think about her own choices. What did she want? And how was she going to get it?

In the bathroom, she waited for a moment to let the shower heat up, then stepped inside. With multiple spray heads, the hot water hit her from all angles. She tried to think of it as therapeutic, washing away the remnants of last night. It had been unbelievably gratifying, both emotionally and physically, but it was over now. There would be no breathless kisses, sexy glances, or flirtation from Astrid. Clay had shut the door and she planned to go out of her way to stay on the other side. Instead, she needed to focus on the one thing she'd done so little of in her first thirty-two years on the planet—figuring out what she truly wanted. Love, family, and career had always been atop the list, and she couldn't deny that those things made real sense in her heart and mind. It was simply time to redouble her efforts.

Clean and shampooed, Astrid shut off the water and climbed out of the shower, wrapping herself up in two of the hotel's fluffy white towels. She took the hair dryer and aimed it at the mirror full-blast to clear the fog. As it receded, she watched her own face come into view. This was what she needed to do—focus on herself and clear away everything that was clouding her judgment. That meant pushing past her desire for Clay.

The trouble was that for the moment, her career goal of establishing herself as an indispensable part of the Sterling team was impossible to reach without Clay. The Seaport project was her most important, and every step of the way was dependent on him. She reminded herself that this wasn't one a one-way proposition. There were two sides to this coin. He needed her, too—to stay on top of the hundreds of tiny details from the city and to keep to the schedule. She would do her job and he would do his. They would succeed together, but with professional distance. It was the only way.

She did not want to return to the dynamic of old, the one where she felt shut out by Clay and every day was a battle of wills. Yes, sex had probably made the next phase of their relationship even more complicated, but those were the cards they had to play with right now. Best to get on with it. Otherwise, she might need to consider other alternatives, like getting on a plane and returning to Norway. She wasn't ready to claim defeat yet.

Clay checked them out while Astrid waited at the valet stand for them to bring his Bentley around. She stood there with her Chloé sunglasses on, staring straight ahead as a parade of expensive cars buzzed by on Sunset Boulevard, wishing she could wiggle her nose and teleport back to San Diego. She was dreading the ride home with Clay.

She slid the valet a generous tip and climbed into the passenger seat while he held the door for her. Clay strode out of the hotel moments later, managing to suck the breath right out of her. He was way too hot, too formidable, tall, and broad. The sight was loudly sounding echoes of last night in her head…his magnificent naked body weighing her down, taking her to new heights, and lavishing her with far more passion than she'd ever dared to imagine. Clay may have given her only one night, but it would be impossible to shake the memory fully. Selfishly, she didn't want to. At least they'd managed to get on the same page for a few hours last night. They'd declared a truce in the most indelible way she could've imagined.

"All set?" Clay asked, fastening his seat belt.

"Yes." Astrid looked straight ahead, unwilling to grant him so much as a smile or even a pleasant glance. She was done with being kind to Clay. Or at least done with going out of her way to offer niceties.

"Would you like to choose some music?" He handed over his phone.

She was tempted to send a message with her selection. Perhaps something desperately sexy and romantic, just to needle him? Or something raw and loud, to mirror the hurt he'd inflicted on her this morning with his preemptive rejection. After all, Astrid hadn't asked for a single thing from him other than to shower together. He'd only assumed that she would want more than that.

She pressed Play on a pithy pop playlist she found in the app's menu. If nothing else, it might wear on him the way his presence wore on her. As he drove, Clay occasionally offered a question or a comment, but otherwise stayed quiet. The purely platonic tone of everything he said was annoying—comments about the weather or traffic or work, but Astrid wasn't about to change the subject. Clay had said his piece back at the hotel—they were colleagues and nothing else. The sooner she got used to this, the better.

As they approached San Diego, Clay seemed to get antsy, fidgeting in his seat.

"Need a bathroom break?" Astrid asked.

His shoulders dropped and he shot her a look. "No. I'm just eager to see my daughter. I'm about to drive past the exit for Miranda's on my way to your place."

"Go get her. Please don't wait on my account.

Trust me, I have nowhere I need to be." *Absolutely nowhere.*

"Are you sure?"

"I would love to meet your daughter. And I always enjoy seeing Miranda." Astrid couldn't ignore what this all meant—it was only after he'd laid down the law that he'd actually considered letting her meet his daughter.

Clay immediately flipped his signal and zipped down the off-ramp to head to Miranda's house. Astrid didn't need yet another thing to admire about Clay. In fact, she was wishing for things to dislike about him, but his frantic desire to see his daughter was nothing short of endearing. Damn him.

Minutes later, they were pulling up in front of Miranda's house, the one she had once shared with Johnathon. Clay had hardly killed the engine before he climbed out of the car and let his long legs carry him to the front door. Astrid wasn't sure what her role was in all of this, and Clay's previous touchiness about Delia made her think it was best if she hung back. If a man was going to be protective of his child, Astrid was not about to stand in the way of that.

Miranda answered the door and caught sight of Astrid, waving to her and casting a smile. Then she disappeared back inside with Clay, leaving the door open. Astrid's stomach twisted with guilt at the secret she was still carrying around, the one about Astrid's tryst with Johnathon when she hadn't realized he had a new love in his life, a woman who just happened to be Miranda. Astrid told herself this was another reason to be glad Clay had set boundaries between them. If the secret came out and Clay learned what had happened, he would never forgive Astrid, even if she had her reasons for keeping it to herself.

Astrid took her time getting to the front door, wanting to afford Clay and his daughter the happy reunion he'd been so eager to have. But when she walked inside the house, she realized she wasn't quite prepared for what it would be like to see this strong man wrapped around the finger of a tiny girl. He had Delia in his arms, her long dark hair flowing in ribbons as he twirled her in a circle.

"Did you miss me?" he asked, using the same nearly unrecognizable tone he'd taken on the phone that morning.

Delia narrowed her eyes on her father's face in much the same way he did at work when he was annoyed by a question Astrid was stupid enough to ask. "Daddy, I told you I did on the phone. Remember?"

"Okay. Okay. I just like hearing it." He pushed her hair back from her face and kissed her cheek. Astrid, still keeping her distance, felt as though her heart was being squeezed tight. Clay was such a different man when he let down his guard. She'd seen it last night and she was witnessing it now that he was around Delia. It was hard to believe he was the same gruff guy she had battled with at work.

Miranda approached the pair and placed her hand on her brother's back. "She did miss you, but not as much as you probably hoped. We had way too much fun."

"We swam in Aunt Miranda's pool and we colored and watched movies and had popcorn."

Clay glanced at Miranda over his shoulder. "Let me guess. You watched *The Snow Princess*."

"Only three times," Miranda answered.

Delia wriggled her way out of her father's arms and pointed at Astrid. "Who are you?"

A look of horror crossed his face. "This is Astrid. She and I work together at Sterling Enterprises."

As if Astrid needed another reminder of the box Clay wanted her to stay in. Astrid stepped closer to Delia, crouching down to get on her level. "I already know who you are. You're the famous Delia. I've heard a lot about you."

A slight smile crossed the little girl's lips, but she seemed to be sizing up Astrid, trying to figure out what she was or where she fit into her life, if at all. "Hi."

Astrid planted her hands on her knees, still stooped down. "So, you like *The Snow Princess*?"

Delia nodded eagerly. "It's my favorite."

"Did you know it's based on a story from Norway?"

"It is? How do you know that?"

Astrid smiled, thinking back to her childhood and the folk tales her brothers used to tell her. They always chose the darkest stories in the hopes of scaring Astrid, but it never worked, and they were confounded. Astrid always wanted to believe the happier parts of those fables. "It's called *The Three Princesses*. The story is different in the movie. It's much more fun."

"Where does the snow come from?"

"There's a lot of snow in Norway and the winter can be very long. That's where I was born and where I grew up."

Delia's eyes went wide. "Really? I've never seen snow in real life. Sometimes you can see it on the mountains around San Diego, but that's not the same."

Clay was carefully watching over their exchange, not letting on as to what he thought of it. "Come on, Delia. Let's get your things packed up. Astrid needs to get home. I'm sure she has a lot she needs to do today."

"Okay." The pair started upstairs, hand in hand.

Astrid couldn't help but feel as though she would only be intruding during the drive home. Clay had made his priorities clear and she couldn't blame him for it. Delia was adorable. Anyone would want to protect her. If she were Astrid's daughter, she would have felt the same way. "Clay? Hold on a minute."

He came to a stop and looked down at her from the top of the stairs, his eyes dark and questioning. "Yes?"

"I'll call a car to take me downtown. You and Delia enjoy the rest of your day together."

Relief washed over his face. He nearly smiled.

Nearly. "Thank you. That would be great. I'll see you at the office on Monday."

Astrid forced a grin. The thought of work soured her stomach. "Yes. Absolutely."

Clay and Delia disappeared up the stairs, leaving Miranda and Astrid downstairs alone.

"So?" Miranda started. "How was it? Do you think that spending that time with my brother will make things easier at work?"

Astrid wasn't quite sure how to answer that question. Nothing about her night with Clay was going to make anything "easier." "We'll see. Your brother is a tough nut to crack."

Miranda nodded. "He always has been. I'm sorry if it's difficult."

Astrid shrugged. "Thank you. I appreciate it." Astrid really had no choice but to soldier through all of this, but she was also starting to wonder if it would ever be worth it. "I wanted to ask if you're available for dinner one night this week. I'd like to have you and Tara over."

"Is this for fun or are we talking business?"

"A little of both. I've just been thinking about my future with Sterling."

Miranda reached for Astrid's arm. "I hope you aren't questioning it because of Clay. I promise he's far more bark than bite."

If only Astrid could tell Miranda what she was really thinking, that Clay had already taken a chunk of her heart and she wasn't sure she could stick around in the hopes of ever reclaiming it. "It's more than your brother. A lot of it's on me." The words echoed in her head. *It's on me.* If she wanted happiness and fulfillment, she had to find it for herself. Not that long ago, she'd thought she'd found a new purpose at Sterling, but the road ahead seemed bumpy at best. She was going to have to hold on tight if she wanted to get past it.

Eight

Astrid arrived at work on Monday morning to a surprise sitting on her desk—a photo of her and Clay from Friday night at the award ceremony. It came with a note from Tara: *You two look great! I hope you had fun.*

Astrid slumped down in her chair and sighed, picking up the photograph and trying to ignore how sad it made her feel. She and Clay looked better than amazing together. They looked like they belonged together. Why did he have to be so deeply opposed to that idea? Did his hurt from his ex-wife really make him that unwilling to ever pursue love? She understood wanting to protect Delia, but surely he realized that all romance involved risk. There was no such thing as a relationship where you didn't ultimately put your heart on the line. She wondered if she'd ever get the chance to tell him that much, or if he would even listen. His stubborn streak was a mile wide and just as deep.

Astrid got to work, deciding to stay in her office and take care of things like paperwork, research, and answering emails. On any other Monday morning, she would have gone in search of Clay so they could regroup on the Seaport project and set the agenda for the week ahead. That would have to happen eventually, but for now, she was going to put it off as long as possible.

A little after noon, she was about to head out to grab a salad for lunch when her cell phone rang with an unfamiliar number on the caller ID.

"Hello?" she answered.

"Ms. Sterling? This is Sandy."

Astrid sat up straighter in her seat and fumbled around the desk for a pen. She wanted to take notes so she could report back to Tara and Miranda. "Oh, hi, Sandy. How are you?"

"I'm good. Really good. You said that morning we ran into each other at the bakery that I could call you."

"Right. Of course. Are you looking for a job? I haven't had a chance to make a formal inquiry into what might be available, but I can certainly do that and get back to you. I would suggest a meeting with

Mr. Singleton so you can discuss your departure. I do think the air needs to be cleared about that."

"I actually don't need a job. I got a new one and it's great. I'm working with the city planner's office. That's why I'm calling."

Astrid had not expected this, and she had to wonder why Sandy would choose to let Astrid know about it. Maybe she was just being paranoid. "Oh. I see."

"I feel bad about the way I left you guys high and dry last time. So I wanted to let you know that if you need anything at all from me, please feel free to ask. I'll be here to answer any questions or provide details about any aspect of the process as we move through the second bidding phase of the project."

"Fantastic." This truly was great news. Astrid's other contact at the city was terrible. She rarely returned Astrid's phone calls and if she did, it was always days later. This could be a real boon for Astrid. "Can I get your direct line?"

"Actually, just use my cell. I called you, so you can grab the number from that. Our phone system here is a nightmare, and that way, you can reach me any time you need me. Even on weekends." Sandy hesitated for a moment. "I did want to let you know that there's been a change to the date for the next pitches. It'll be Friday, November 13, rather than the sixth."

Astrid scribbled more notes. "Wow. So we have an extra week?"

"Yes. One person on the committee had to take some time off with a sick relative. We thought we should give everyone some extra time. There will be a longer wait after this round until we announce the firm that will actually get the project. It won't happen now until after Christmas."

That would be a long wait. The original schedule had it slated to be announced before the holidays. Apparently, Astrid would be staying in San Diego until at least January. Then she could decide if Sterling was a place where she had a real future or if it might be better to return home to Norway. "I see. Well, thank you so much for the update. I really appreciate it."

"My pleasure, Mrs. Sterling. I do have one more bit of information though, and I'm afraid it isn't good news. I know that Sterling had inquired about naming the park that will be on site after Johnathon Sterling, but I'm afraid that just won't be possible. The city will be retaining naming rights."

That made perfect sense to Astrid. Things like stadiums and museums and concert halls all had some sort of corporate affiliation now. There was simply too much money to be made. "I understand. Better to know now rather than later. Thank you for letting me know."

"No problem. I'm going to get going, but I guess I'll talk to you soon."

"Bye." Astrid hung up and knew that she was going to have to relay this information to Clay. Best to do it now and get it over with. She strode down the hall to his office, poking her head inside. He was at his drafting table, with his back to the door, headphones on. He often listened to music when he was working. Jazz, mostly. He said it helped him concentrate and create at the same time.

Not wanting to surprise him, she knocked firmly on his door, but apparently the music was too loud. With no other option, she tapped him on the shoulder, then hopped back. Sure enough, he jumped. He grabbed the headphones and pulled them from his head, plopping them on the table. "Astrid. You surprised me."

"I'm sorry. I knocked, but you didn't hear me."

He drew in a deep breath through his nose, but avoided eye contact. Apparently things were going to be awkward for a while. "Can I help you with something?"

"I heard from Sandy. Tara's old assistant? You'll never guess where she's working. The city planner's office."

"Good for her." He walked over to his desk and sat, waking up his computer.

"Do you not understand what I'm saying? We now have a direct line of communication with them. Hopefully that will mean less red tape, which should make things easier on us both. In fact, she called to tell me the deadline has been pushed back a week because of some internal scheduling issues."

"I guess that's good."

Astrid was so frustrated she was about to scream, and she was tired of hiding these emotions. She planted both of her hands on his desk. "Are you going to look at me, Clay? Are you going to engage in actual conversation with me?"

His jaw tensed, but he finally looked up at her. "Astrid, I'm trying my best, okay? I just think that it's better for both of us if we keep some distance at work."

"That would be nice if we weren't working on the same crucial project, but we are. And again, just as I told you in LA, you don't need to take everything so seriously. If we're done, we're done. Let's move on." She was going to have to repeat those words to herself until she began to believe them. But that was a problem she would keep to herself.

Clay got up from his desk, looked out in the hall, then closed the door behind him. Astrid couldn't help it, but knowing that they were alone made her stomach do a somersault.

"Miranda knows." Clay crossed his arms over his chest, which was its own distraction—the way it made his upper arms strain was a little too alluring.

"Wait. What? How?" Astrid couldn't imagine how they possibly could have given themselves up when they'd gone to Miranda's house that afternoon. They'd been so careful. Clay had gone out of his way to keep his distance.

"I really don't want to talk about this right now.

Not in the middle of the day in the office. There are too many loose lips."

He was right on the money about that. "Okay. Well, I'm guessing you don't want to tell me over a drink or dinner."

"That's probably not a great idea." He ran his hand through his hair. Astrid wished she could be doing that right now. She wished everything standing between them would just go away. "Let's talk at six, when most people are gone. I'll get the nanny to stay late with Delia."

"It's that serious? Why can't you just tell me how Miranda knows?"

"There's more to it than that. I feel like I need to explain myself."

Astrid wasn't sure what to think anymore. "Okay, then. I'll be back at six."

Clay was watching the clock. Astrid was always on time for everything, and he had a feeling tonight would be no exception. He didn't relish telling her the things he was about to. He didn't go about laying his soul bare. It was easier if her kept it all inside and hidden. That way, no one could use his feelings against him.

But after Miranda deduced what had happened in Los Angeles, and after she'd found out that he'd ended things with Astrid then and there, Miranda had insisted. She said that at the very least, Astrid deserved a full explanation of why he felt the way he did. Miranda had also tried to encourage him to give Astrid another chance. He wasn't sure he could do that. It didn't seem smart, especially after he'd already done the hard part and cut things off. Still, he did rely on his sister for guidance when it came to matters of the heart. She had a way of getting to the root of things, and most important, she understood him like no one else.

Astrid appeared in his doorway at 6:02, smiling wide and holding a recognizable bag from the bakery across the street. "They're all sold out of doughnuts this late in the day, but they just pulled some of those monster chocolate chip cookies out of the oven. If we're going to have a big talk, I figured sugar might lighten the mood."

For what felt like the one hundredth time, he felt as though he was stuck in the role of the beast while she was the kindhearted beauty. "Thank you so much. I could definitely use a pick-me-up." He went to his office door and closed it behind Astrid. The click of the latch made it all seem more real. He had to come clean. "Can I get you something to drink?" Clay had a fully stocked mini-fridge in his office. It had been his only request when they'd designed his office.

"Water is fine."

Clay retrieved two bottles and handed one to her. Drinking in the office might be a relic of the 1950s and '60s, but Clay could see the appeal right now. A finger or two of bourbon might make this easier.

He joined Astrid on the couch, sitting at the opposite end. She turned to face him, pulling her leg up onto the cushion between them. "I think we should start with how your sister found out what happened. I can't see where we could've possibly tipped our hand at her house." As if to soften the blow of the topic, she handed over the bakery bag after pulling out a cookie for herself.

"When I was video chatting with Miranda and Delia, I sat in the chair in the corner of the room and you got up to walk to the bathroom. There was a mirror behind me and she saw your naked reflection. It was only a split second, but she saw it." He'd been so distracted, he hadn't noticed it at all, but then again, he'd had the real thing right in his field of view.

"You don't think Delia saw me, do you? That would be horrible." She took an anxious bite of her cookie.

"I asked Miranda that same question, but she's pretty sure Delia would've said something."

"Okay, good." Astrid cracked open her water and took a long drink.

Clay tried hard not to fixate on the curve of her lips around the opening of the bottle, and instead focused on his cookie, which was impossibly good but still not as appealing as Astrid. "Miranda and I talked for a bit after you left, and after she told me she knew what had happened. Delia was occupied with saying goodbye to the fish in Miranda's aquarium."

Astrid stuck out her lower lip. "That's adorable."

"I know. It is." Astrid wasn't making this any easier. He brushed away a piece of lint on his trouser leg, searching for words. "Miranda didn't want to let it go because I told her before we went to Los Angeles that I was struggling with my attraction to you and I didn't want anything to happen."

Her eyes flashed as if she was trying to solve a mystery and she'd just had her "aha" moment. "Was that why you were angry when we ended up in the same room?"

"I wouldn't say I was angry."

"Annoyed. Miffed. Irked. Those are all emotions you direct at me."

He sat forward and rested his elbows on his thighs, running his hands up over his face and back through his hair. "I know. I'm sorry I do that. It's just that…"

"I don't need your apologies. I just want to know what's really going on here. This feels like so much more than the fact that we work together. It feels like so much more than you not wanting to get involved. So, please. Explain it to me so I can understand."

"I can't bring myself to trust a woman again, Astrid."

"That's it?"

"That's the essence of it, yes. My ex-wife destroyed any faith I ever had in love, which wasn't much to begin with. You know, Miranda and I have been on our own since we were young. Our mother left us with our grandmother, who was furious that her only daughter stuck her with such a huge responsibility."

"I didn't know about that." Her voice was so soft and understanding, it nearly broke his heart.

"But, somehow, I fell in love when I met my ex-wife. Or at least I thought it was love. Obviously it wasn't, because she left, too. And when she did, she took my trust and Delia's along with it." The emotion was welling up inside him, threatening to overflow. He wouldn't let it. He had to stay in control. But still, it was easier if he kept directing his stare down at the carpet. One look at Astrid and it would be all over. "Do you have any idea how confused Delia was? The number of times she woke up in the middle of the night and wanted her mom and all she had was me? As hard as my childhood was, that was harder, and that was all while I was trying to get over a broken heart."

Astrid scooted closer on the couch and placed her hand on his shoulder. "You really loved her, didn't you?"

"I did. She was everything. She was sweet and kind and beautiful. She was generous and giving." There it was. There was the essence of what was eating away at him from the inside. He turned his head and felt brave enough to look Astrid in the eye. "She was so much like you. Or at least she pretended to be. At first."

Astrid froze for a moment and dropped her head, then pinched the bridge of her nose as if she had the worst headache in the world. He knew he was doing that to her and the realization killed him. "I'm not your ex-wife, Clay. If I seem to have some of the same qualities, I'm not the same person. I could never, ever do the things that she did. Lying to my husband? Stealing his money? Leaving behind my child? Never."

"So you know the whole story. I don't even have to tell you." He sat back in his seat and shook his head. Here he'd thought he would need to come clean and she already knew.

"I didn't know about your mom. Miranda told me the rest. The night she helped me pick out my dress. It was only because she cares about you so deeply. I didn't say anything because you don't like it when I get too personal."

"And then I went and made things extra personal the other night." Should he be regretting his decision to sleep with Astrid? He didn't want to.

"No. We both did that. I wanted that. I needed it." She took his hand and pulled it into her lap, stroking his palm with her fingers. "I don't regret it. I won't. I refuse." She sucked in a breath so deep it made her shoulders rise up around her ears. "But it did mean something to me. It meant a lot. When I tried to act all nonchalant the next morning, that was a lie. That wasn't what I was really thinking." Her wide eyes scanned his face, as if she was looking for some sort of answer.

"If we can't be honest with each other, I don't see how we could ever be involved."

"I was protecting myself. You're doing the same thing. I don't see a difference. Would it have made it easier that morning if I had protested? Begged you to want more from me? I won't do that, Clay. I do have some self-respect." She got up from the sofa, dropped the second half of her cookie in the bakery bag and threw it in the trash. "Maybe this was all a mistake. Maybe we need to accept that and move on."

"I hate that word. *Mistake*."

"And yet you use it all the time. I'm guessing it's gone through your head many times as pertains to me."

"If anyone made a mistake, it was me."

She shook her head in disbelief. There was also some disdain mixed in with her expression. This was what he deserved—her scorn. "Thanks. That makes me feel even worse." She reached for the doorknob and he bolted up from the couch.

"Astrid. Wait. Stop."

She turned her head so fast her hair whipped in the air. "What?"

"I'm sorry."

"Again, I don't want apologies."

"Then what do you want?"

Her eyes softened. "I've asked myself that question many times since Friday night. And I'm still not entirely sure of the full answer, but I do know a few things. I want a family. I want a career. And I want love. Real, passionate, unquestioning love. I want the sort of love that lasts. Forever. I know now how hurt you have been. And I appreciate that. But I've been hurt, too. And I'm not going to put my heart on the line for someone who simply isn't capable of returning my feelings. You aren't the only one with skin in the game."

Clay held his breath. She was right. So damn right. And he was a fool. "I know that. I do."

She let out another exasperated sigh. "I care about you, Clay. But I think this is another illustration of how infrequently you and I are on the same page. So perhaps we should focus on work, since that's the part of our relationship that impacts other people. Let's try to get along and get through the Seaport project. As near as I can see, that's our best case scenario."

It didn't sound like much of a best case to him, but he didn't have a retort. He'd stirred up the confusion, and he was the person always arguing for a sensible course of action. Astrid's idea was practical. Logical. Nobody would get hurt. "I agree. You're right."

"Bye, Clay. I'll see you tomorrow." Astrid opened the door and marched out of his office.

He leaned against the jamb and watched as she walked away. He'd hoped he might feel better after opening up. Instead, he felt as though he was right back where he was before he and Astrid ever went to Los Angeles.

Nine

It had been a hell of a week and it was only Thursday. Astrid couldn't stop thinking about her conversation with Clay and everything he had been through. She liked him—a lot—but did she really want that much trouble in her life? Her existence with Johnathon had been hard. Years of vying for his attention and affection, month after month of infertility treatments, and ultimately, the realization that the love between them turned into something far less warm and caring than she ever would have wanted. What if that happened again?

At work, she and Clay had returned to their old dynamic, but there was a layer of unease in the air that hadn't been there before. That was saying a lot—

their interactions before LA had been plenty uncomfortable at times. Perhaps it was all in her head and Clay wasn't thinking about her at all, or about the things she'd lobbed back in his court. She hoped that wasn't the case and that he'd taken at least *some* of it to heart. Yes, he had been hurt, badly. But he wasn't the only one carrying around battle scars. At some point, he was going to have to admit that he might not be protecting his heart. He might be slowly smothering it to death.

For tonight, Astrid would have a distraction from her turmoil over Clay. Tara and Miranda were coming over for dinner. That was fraught with its own complications. Miranda had figured out what happened between Astrid and Clay. Astrid was legitimately surprised she hadn't received a phone call about it during the week, but she was certain that meant it was going to come up in conversation. With Tara there, Astrid wasn't sure how it would all shake out.

Tonight would mark the first time the wives had ever met at Astrid's penthouse apartment in downtown San Diego. All previous gatherings of the three wives had happened at Tara's or Miranda's, aside from the times they'd convened at places like Ruby's to shop for Astrid's dress, or on much sadder occasions like Johnathon's funeral or the lawyer's office for the reading of his will.

That day seemed as though it had happened a decade ago, but it had only been a few months. Astrid had never bargained on becoming business partners with either of them, let alone both, but that had been exactly what happened when Johnathon split his shares of Sterling Enterprises between them. For the most part, she liked Tara and Miranda very much, and she was grateful that he had managed to bring them together after his death. Was that what he had always wanted? For the three of them to be friends? She could see his ego trying to engineer that—three women he'd once loved, united because of him. In her mind, it was an awfully prideful pursuit, but that was Johnathon—he bent the world to suit his needs. Astrid needed to take a page out of Johnathon's book and start doing the same for herself.

Astrid's personal chef had come over yesterday to prepare tonight's meal, which she merely had to heat and serve. On the menu was honey-glazed salmon with roasted vegetables. For dessert, they had chocolate mousse. Astrid didn't believe in not satisfying her sweet tooth every chance she got. Life was too short.

Tara and Miranda arrived together, Tara with a bottle of wine. She was dressed in all black—silk blouse and tailored trousers, an elegant ensemble that made her look every bit the powerful and in-control woman. "I wasn't sure what you were serving, but I figured we couldn't go wrong with a nice chablis."

Astrid accepted the gift, instantly recognizing the label. "Oh, I love this wine. Johnny took me to the winery every time we went to France. He loved it there."

"It's so cute when you call him Johnny." Miranda looked radiant in a plum-colored dress that showed off her raven hair and her growing baby bump.

Astrid was embarrassed. "It's an old habit I need to get rid of. No one else called him that."

Miranda smiled and patted Astrid's shoulder. "I understand. We all have our special memories of Johnathon. For me, one was that winery in France." She gestured to the wine bottle. "Because he took me there, too."

"Same," Tara said. "And for the record, he found out about the winery from me. I was the wine aficionado in our marriage."

The three wives exchanged knowing glances. It did feel as though they were learning new things about Johnathon all the time, simply from spending so much time together.

"Interesting. He always framed himself as the expert." Astrid led them into the heart of her apartment, with its open floor plan, high ceilings, and admittedly unpractical color scheme of nothing but white and cream. She had everything she could ever want here, a spacious living space, a formal dining room, and state-of-the-art gourmet kitchen. There was only one bedroom, but it was a generous size and so comfortably appointed with high thread-count bedding in shades of cream and pale gray that Astrid sometimes referred to as her cocoon. It had a spa-like bathroom with a separate shower and a two-person soaking tub, plus a walk-in closet even she had a difficult time filling. Still, as perfect as her home was, it was a solitary existence living alone perched atop a skyscraper. She sometimes felt like a princess shut away in a tower.

"Your place is stunning." Miranda was drawn to the windows at the far side of the apartment. On the twentieth floor, it had incredible views of the city and the bay, especially at night, when lights twinkled like diamonds against the backdrop of an night sky.

"Thank you. Johnathon bought it for me soon after we started dating. He wanted me in San Diego more often, but I wasn't about to move in with him when we'd only known each other for a month. Now that I look back on it, it seems a little crazy."

Miranda nodded and turned back to Astrid. "He did like to push things along quickly, didn't he? I felt like our courtship was so fast. We were dating, then we were engaged and married, all within six months."

Astrid's stomach soured, just thinking about that particular sequence of events. Somewhere in the midst of that, Johnathon flew to Norway and seduced Astrid, without saying a peep about his new love.

"I think he took things faster as he got older," Tara offered. "We dated for over a year before he popped the question. Now I know that some of that had to do with Grant."

"Really?" Miranda asked, taking a seat on the white linen sofa in Astrid's living room.

"I'll get the wineglasses while Tara tells us this story. I want to hear every last thing. Miranda, what can I get you to drink?"

"Sparkling water, if you have it."

"Coming right up." Astrid ventured to the wet bar on the opposite side of the room, first serving Miranda's drink before opening the wine and pouring herself and Tara each a glass. She joined Miranda on the couch while Tara sat in one of two high-backed upholstered chairs.

"You know, I met Grant and Johnathon the same night," Tara said.

"I guess I didn't know that," Miranda said.

"Grant and I had serious sparks, but Johnathon was the one who pursued me, so I figured that my connection with Grant was all in my imagination. I didn't know this until recently, but he and Johnathon butted heads about it several times. We're talking very heated arguments. That's part of why I got forced out of Sterling Enterprises at the beginning. Grant told Johnathon that he couldn't work with both of us, and of course, Johnathon wasn't about to get rid of his best friend. I was already his wife. I wasn't going anywhere."

"So guilt was the reason he gave you a third of his shares in the company?" Miranda said coolly. She'd made it clear from the beginning that she felt Johnathon had shortchanged her.

"I take it that still bothers you?" Tara asked.

"Well, of course it does, but my beef is with Johnathon, not with you two. I really appreciate that we've found a way to come together." She took a sip of her sparkling water and set the glass back down on the coffee table. "I don't have any family other than Clay and Delia. I don't have more than a handful of close friends. The interior design business is incredibly competitive. People will be nice to your face and then they'll stab you in the back. It might be counterintuitive, but I trust you two. I guess it's because Johnathon trusted you, too."

The guilt was bearing down on Astrid with unrelenting force. If Miranda trusted her now, it would be destroyed if Astrid's secret was ever revealed. Perhaps it would be better if she simply came out with it. But then again, it would cause so much pain. Miranda would feel betrayed by the man whose baby she was carrying and that could never be resolved. She'd never be able to speak to him and work it out, find out why he'd done what he'd done. It would forever change her image of the man she had loved so greatly. Astrid took a deep breath and a healthy gulp of her wine. No, she would live with the secret and keep it from hurting anyone else.

Her secret aside, Astrid had a different unpleasant topic she had to bring up. "Since we're discussing Johnathon, I'm afraid I have to let you both know that we can't name the Seaport park after him if we get the project. The city is retaining naming rights."

"That's not terribly surprising," Tara said.

"It's still disappointing." Miranda placed her hand on her belly. "I had visions of taking the baby to that park, and being able to tell them that it was named after their father."

Astrid could hear the heartbreak in Miranda's voice. They were all still grieving, but Miranda was the closest to the loss. "I'm sorry. I really am. If there was anything I could do about it, I would have."

Miranda sniffled, but nodded. "I know you would have. I don't blame you."

The timer went off in the kitchen. "That's dinner," Astrid said. "If you two want to take your seats at the dining table, I'll bring it out."

"I'm going to run to the ladies' room first," Miranda said.

"Down the hall on the left." Astrid got up from her seat and headed into the kitchen.

Tara trailed behind Astrid. "Let me help."

Astrid was putting on a pair of oven mitts. "The plates are right there." With a nod she gestured to the kitchen island. She pulled out a large sheet pan and set it on a trivet. "Tara, can we talk about something?"

"Of course." Tara watched as Astrid removed foil from their meal, steam billowing in the air. "That looks and smells amazing."

"Thanks. My chef made it for us."

"What did you want to talk to me about?" Tara leaned back against the counter.

"Remember the day you introduced me to Clay and I saw the picture from Miranda and Johnathon's wedding?"

Tara's eyes went wide. "And everything you told me afterward?"

Thank God Astrid didn't have to explain it further. "Yes. That."

"What about it?"

"I just want to be sure we will always keep it between us."

"Oh, of course." Tara stole a roasted carrot from the pan. "That needs to be forgotten. Someone will just get hurt."

"Who's getting hurt?" Miranda appeared in the kitchen doorway.

"Nobody," Tara and Astrid said, nearly in unison.

"Then what were you talking about?"

"There's a paper shredder in the office that has a mind of its own," Tara blurted, somewhat unconvincingly.

"Then throw it out." Miranda narrowed her sights on Tara.

"Smart. We'll do that."

Astrid could finally exhale. "Everyone hungry? I think this is going to be good."

"I'm starving," Miranda said.

"Good. Because we have tons of food." Astrid dished up each plate and they took them to the dining table. Astrid appreciated that she could keep things informal with Tara and Miranda.

Tara raised her wineglass for a toast. "To Johnathon Sterling's three wives. May we always get along."

Miranda laughed and shook her head. "That's not particularly optimistic."

Tara shrugged. "You never know what's going to happen."

Astrid knocked back the last of her first glass of wine and poured herself a refill. Tonight might be a big test of her nerves.

"So, Astrid. Any highlights from your trip to Los Angeles you care to share?" Miranda asked the question with a tone that said Astrid had better spill it.

Okay, then. That had happened lightning fast. "You're talking about me and Clay?"

"Yes." Miranda nodded then took a bite of her salmon. "Delicious."

"Did I miss something?" Tara asked.

"You could say that." Miranda jumped in with response before Astrid had a chance.

"You two weren't arguing on that trip, were you? I honestly don't understand it."

Astrid was desperate to take control of the conversation. This game was grating on her nerves. "Clay and I slept together." She shot a pointed look at Miranda, then Tara, before stabbing a sweet potato with her fork. Astrid kept herself composed, hoping to hell that neither of them would ask for details.

"What happened?" Tara asked.

Well, that didn't last for very long. "Part of it was

because we ended up in the same hotel room. You said you were going to put us in separate rooms, but that's not what the hotel had for us when we arrived."

"That's your excuse?" Tara set down her napkin. "You're a shareholder in the company and you slept with one of your coworkers?"

Astrid shot her a pointed stare, doing her best to convey just how ridiculous Tara was being right now. "Are you kidding me? What about you and Grant? One could argue that was far worse. You two were both in positions of power, and you didn't do a very good job of hiding it, either. At least I didn't kiss someone on the Kiss Cam at a Major League baseball game."

"Grant and I have history. And we're engaged now."

"Astrid's right, Tara. You did the same thing," Miranda said. "And you put our mutual interest in the company at much greater risk."

Astrid didn't want to gang up on Tara, but she did appreciate that Miranda had her back. "I really don't think either of us is in a position to throw stones right now."

"Obviously I wasn't there, but I have a feeling it didn't happen simply because you two were in the same room. Judging by the conversation I had with Clay before you two went to LA, I'm guessing it would have happened even if you'd been at completely different hotels," Miranda said.

"So I heard," Astrid said.

Now it was Miranda's turn to be surprised. "He told you?"

"He did. And we had a long conversation about why he called things off the next morning."

"Wow," Miranda said. "He actually listened to what I said."

"I don't know exactly what you told him to do, but we did have a heart-to-heart. I think we understand each other better." She was still guessing at these things. There was nothing certain about Clay.

"Where did you leave things?" Tara asked.

"Are you asking me as a shareholder and co-CEO of Sterling Enterprises, or are you asking as a girlfriend?"

Tara waited a moment to answer, buying time with two sips of her wine. "Since it's just the three of us and we're off the clock, I guess I'm asking as a friend."

"We agreed that it was a one-time thing. That was it. We're both single and we were caught up in the excitement of his big win. But it wasn't anything more than sex." Except that it had been, at least for Astrid. She needed to banish those thoughts from her mind, immediately. All they did was make her want Clay more. "And we also agreed that we would keep it quiet. Obviously that didn't work here, but I hope I can trust you both to keep it to yourselves."

"In my experience, the 'it was only sex' excuse doesn't hold water. Especially if you have to keep working together," Tara said. "Is this going to interfere with the Seaport project? Or anything else for that matter?"

"It won't. We're back to being strictly platonic. I swear. There isn't even a glimmer of flirtation between us."

"That's a little disappointing," Miranda said.

"It is?" Tara asked.

"Yes. I mean, come on. Sterling is going to be fine, whether or not two of its employees become romantically involved. The world isn't going to suddenly stop needing new office buildings or corporate campuses." Miranda sat back in her seat. "But I am worried about my brother and what kind of life he's living right now. He's lonely. I know he is. And he's a little lost, to be honest. I'd love it if he found a partner who could help steer him in the right direction. Someone who could make him happy."

"Are you attempting to play matchmaker here, Miranda?" Tara asked.

"I guess I am. Astrid is great and I love my brother, so I fail to see how that could be a bad thing."

Astrid felt stuck. She loved having Miranda's endorsement and she believed that Miranda was right about Clay. He *did* need love in his life. But this was also a lot of pressure to put on Astrid. She couldn't fix Clay. He had to do it himself. "I don't know if he believes that I could, in fact, make him happy. And to be honest, I'm not sure of my ability to do that, either. We don't know each other that well, and I don't know how to change that. We agreed to keep things strictly professional at work, and from the company's standpoint, that's the best course. I can't see him agreeing to see me socially, and I'm not about to ask, just so I can be rejected."

"Then let's make an opportunity. Surely we can think of something between the three of us?"

"A party to celebrate his award?" Tara offered. "We could invite the press. Turn it into some publicity for Sterling."

"I really don't think he would go for that," Astrid said. "He hates parties."

"I agree," Miranda echoed Astrid's assertion. "But I do have another idea."

"Let's hear it," Tara said.

"I found out the baby's gender this week. Well, I didn't find out. The doctor wrote it down and it's in a sealed envelope. Everyone's doing those gender reveal parties now, and with Johnathon gone, I don't want to find out on my own. I'd rather have people I care about with me."

"That sounds like fun," Astrid said. "I'd love to host." With so little social life, it would give her something to do. Plus, she wanted to let Clay into her world, and show him who she was.

"I read in a magazine about a couple who gave their results to a baker who filled cupcakes with blue or pink frosting. The guests all took a bite at the same time to find out the gender," Miranda said.

"If baked goods are involved, you will have no problem convincing Clay to be here," Astrid said.

Miranda laughed. "That is so true."

"I love the whole idea," Tara added. "I'm sure Grant would love it, too."

"I do think we should at least toast to Clay's award," Astrid said. "He doesn't like to be in the spotlight, but he deserves it."

"So much. Let's make it an evening event, too. It's more romantic." Miranda punctuated her suggestion with a wink.

Astrid grinned, looking at Tara and Miranda, thankful for this unlikely sisterhood she'd found. "So are we doing this?"

"Yes. I think so. If you plan the whole thing, I'll be sure to get my brother here."

Ten

A small, intimate gathering should not be stressful. And yet, Astrid was a ball of nerves. It went beyond the fact that it had been a crazy busy week at work and she'd spent too little time arranging the small details of this party.

Honestly, this whole idea was a bit absurd, that she and Clay would somehow grow closer over the course of the next few hours. But it seemed as though it was worth trying, and she had wanted to celebrate the baby on the way in some public way for a while now. She simply didn't know how to bring up the topic. She and Miranda were still forging their bond.

Astrid read through the instructions her private chef had left for the food to be served. Just a few hot appetizers, along with a cheese board and veggies. The cupcakes, with the mystery filling, were already on site, sitting on the kitchen counter. Really, everything was set, and she only needed to shower, get dressed and take a deep breath.

The bell for her apartment door rang, but it was a little less than two hours until guests were to arrive. There was only one other apartment up on the top floor of her building, so it was rare to get unannounced visitors, but she had left her guest list with the doorman already. Perhaps it was Tara or Miranda stopping by to say hello. She opened the door, and there before her was Clay, looking good enough to eat in black trousers and a crisp gray shirt, with a bouquet of pink tulips in his hand. Astrid practically swooned.

He surveyed her from head to toe, his forehead wrinkling with confusion, probably because she was in jeans and a light sweater at the moment. "Am I early?"

"Yes, actually. By nearly two hours."

"Miranda told me it started at five."

So that was what this was—a ploy by Miranda to get them together. Astrid approved. And also felt the need to cover for her. "We talked about five at one point, but I moved it to seven. I'm so sorry she didn't tell you."

"Should I come back?"

Astrid shook her head and grasped his arm. "Don't be silly. You can keep me company."

"Oh. Okay." Clay walked inside and Astrid closed the door behind him. He was quick to thrust the flowers at her. "Here. These are for you. I thought about a bottle of wine, but the truth is that I'm really a bourbon guy, and that seemed like an odd hostess gift."

Astrid smiled. They might not be a romantic gesture, but she loved getting flowers from Clay. "Thank you so much. Tulips are my favorite."

"I noticed that you sometimes have them in your office."

Wow. "Careful, Clay. That's downright thoughtful of you."

He leaned against the kitchen counter. As perfect as they'd looked together in that photo from the night in Los Angeles, she thought he looked even more perfect in her apartment. "Actually, it's good that I got here early. I've been wanting to talk to you about our chat the other night at work."

She had no idea what he was about to say, but she was glad he'd been thinking about it. She'd been stuck with a nonstop loop of their conversation in her head. "Of course."

"I wanted to say thank you for being so understanding and listening to me. I also want to thank you for calling me out on a few things. I love my sister, and she does tell me when I'm wrong, but she also probably gives me a little too much latitude."

"Does that mean you've changed your mind about what you will allow to happen in your romantic life?"

She might as well put it all on the line. Better to know now what he was thinking.

"Let's just say that my hard-lined approach might be softening." He had a sly glint in his eye that made Astrid's heart flutter.

She didn't want to take too much latitude right now and spook him, but this revelation did make her feel more optimistic about the way this night might go. "Any interest in helping me wrap a gift for your sister?"

"I didn't know we were doing gifts."

"We aren't, technically. But she mentioned this specific thing and I had to get it for her, but it's going to be impossible to wrap. It's a pretty big job, but since you're an architect, I'm thinking you're up to the task."

He seemed skeptical. "That hardly sounds like a job I'm qualified for."

"Come on." Astrid led Clay through her living room and back to her bedroom, where the gift was waiting. "There. I need to figure out how to wrap that."

Clay looked at her as if she had a screw loose. "You can't wrap a stroller."

"Why not?"

He walked over to it and gave it a push across the hardwood floor. How did he manage to make the role of dad so super sexy? "I don't know. Because it's ridiculous? Just put a bow on it."

"Don't you think it would be funny? If we bring

it out to Miranda and it's obvious what it is, but it's still wrapped?"

He regarded the stroller and let out a quiet laugh. "I guess."

"Look, I want tonight to be special for your sister. Just help me, okay?" She stepped to the corner and grabbed the extra-large roll of heavy-duty wrapping paper she'd bought, then handed Clay the scissors and tape.

"Alright then, let's get to work." Together, on hands and knees, they wrapped every square inch of the thing—the handle, the frame and seat, and even the wheels. It required a lot of tape and a lot of one person holding the paper in place while the other made sure it all stuck together. At nearly every juncture there was a brush of hands. The bumping of shoulders. The exchange of smiles. Each time they made contact, the hunger inside her grew a little more, as Astrid was hit with a different memory of her night with Clay. The raw passion of the first time. His mouth on her body. Her hands all over his.

"I have to ask you," Clay said when they were nearly finished. "Why would you host a baby-related event for my sister? For that matter, why buy her an expensive gift? Doesn't it hurt, considering that you and Johnathon tried to have a baby and it didn't happen for you?"

Astrid sat back on her haunches. "You know about that?"

"I do. You hinted at it in the car on the way to LA, and my sister mentioned it as well."

"Ah, Miranda. She does enjoy sharing people's stories, doesn't she?"

His eyes, so warm and welcoming in the soft light of her bedroom, settled on her face. "She does when she cares about someone. Believe me, everything she said was only in the context of marveling at your generosity. She was genuinely surprised at how you took the news of her pregnancy. I think it means a great deal to her."

"And there's your answer. It doesn't hurt to help her celebrate. We're still welcoming a baby into the world, and this baby is special. He or she will be one half someone I loved very much. Plus, I can't help but be excited by the idea of all children. That's part of why I've always wanted to be a mom."

"That is the sweetest thing I have ever heard." His voice was low and soft, and she sensed now that there was an invisible tether between them. There was a reason she was so drawn to him. "How are you so amazing? Are you even real?"

She would have laughed if the question wasn't putting her on a pedestal she never asked for. "Of course I am. I'm flesh and blood like anyone else. I'm just as breakable as anyone." She didn't want to cry, but as her sights traveled between Clay and the stroller, all she could think about was what might have been, both in her distant past and the more recent. She and Clay could have been something. They could still be something, if he'd only let her in. A tear leaked from her eye and she quickly swiped it away.

"I didn't mean to upset you."

"I'm fine," she lied.

Clay spread his arms wide. "No, you're not. Come here."

"No. I'm not going to cry."

He tilted his head to one side, waving her closer with his hand. "Astrid. Come on. I'm not going to think any less of you."

"It's not that." She turned to confront him, frustrated that she wanted him so badly. "It's that I want happy things between you and me. We've both been hurt. We've both had pain. I want to focus on what's good between us. Just us. Nobody else."

"Okay. I can do that."

"Can you, Clay? Can you really?"

He nodded eagerly. "Of course I can."

"Then show me. Do something that will make us both happy."

"Don't you have guests coming in an hour and a half?"

Boundaries. Limitations. Rules. The man was so damn preoccupied with everything that wouldn't allow them to enjoy each other. "Stop telling me no, Clay. I just want to hear you say yes."

A knowing smile slowly rolled across Clay's tempting lips. "Let me figure out how many ways I can say it." He reached for her hair, gently combing through the strands about her ear. He trailed his fingers along her jaw, sending goose bumps racing over the surface of her skin. That right there was the reason she always wanted Clay to say yes to her—there was no match for the thrill of his touch. He caressed her lower lip with his thumb, lifting her chin. She smiled as she snaked his arm around her waist, tugged her hard against his firm body.

This was going to happen again and she hoped to hell this time wouldn't be the last.

Clay had wanted this moment since they'd left LA. He'd just been too conflicted to admit it. And now that it was hurtling at him, getting Astrid into bed wasn't happening fast enough. His pants were so tight he wasn't sure how he was still breathing, let alone still upright. He had to have her, body and soul, now. Heat raged inside him, his erection already fierce and insistent.

She walked backward to the bed, pulling him along with her. He grabbed the hem of her sweater and lifted it above her head. It felt as though he was revealing his reward, a prize he wanted all for himself. He kissed her and unhooked her bra, admiring her beautiful breasts before giving them a squeeze. Her eyes drifted shut halfway, and the pure ecstasy of her expression made him want to do that to her again and again. He unbuttoned her jeans and pulled them down her legs, stopping to kneel before her, gazing up at the beautiful length of her body.

He dotted her belly with soft, openmouthed kisses

as he tugged her panties past her hips. "Lie down, Astrid." He stood as she climbed onto the bed and stretched out before him.

"What about you? You need to take your clothes off."

He did. He really did need to do that, but his mouth and hands were telling him to wait just one more minute. He placed one knee on the bed and gathered her wrists in one hand, raising her arms up above her head. "Are you alright?" he asked, stealing a kiss.

"Perfect," she replied.

He lowered his mouth to one of her breasts, her velvety skin nearly melting into his touch, conforming to his lips. Her nipples were tight and pert, and every time he touched them, her skin flooded with warmth.

He stood. "Don't move. Keep your hands where they are."

A gorgeous smile spread across her lips as she wriggled in place on the bed. He shucked his shirt, pants and boxers, watching her as she watched him.

"You're magnificent with no clothes on. You know that, right?" she asked.

"I'd say the exact same thing of you." He'd never craved a woman the way he did her, as if he could spend the rest of his life exploring her and he'd never stop learning and admiring. He stood with his knees pressed against the side of the bed and lifted her leg, holding her ankle, trailing the back of his other hand along the creamy skin of her inner thigh. He knew they were on a strict timetable here, but it was impossible to not want to take his time. "Can we call your doorman and tell him not to let anyone else up to your apartment?"

"You're terrible."

He bounced his eyebrows up and down. "I hope not." He again placed a knee on the mattress, and bracketed her hips with his legs, reaching up with one hand and holding her wrists in place above her head. His heart was in his throat, knowing he had her under his control. With every passing second, with every pump of blood through his body, she further occupied his heart. She could have had absolutely anything from him. Absolutely anything.

He shifted above her, lowering his head and kissing her deeply, then moving to her jaw, her slender throat, and then kissed the tender undersides of her breasts, coaxing breaths out of her. He traveled down her, milling with his lips, the kisses becoming deeper and longer. She sucked in a sharp breath when he palmed her thighs and spread her legs wide. Then he kissed her apex and he seized control again, exploring her most delicate places with his tongue and lips. He knew what he was doing, but he still loved hearing her reaction to it, the way her breaths stopped and started.

Her hips bucked off the bed as his tongue traveled in circles. She dug her hands into his hair. "That feels so amazing, but I need you. Right now. I need you to make love to me."

He took a few more passes, just enough to show her how dedicated he was to making sure she enjoyed this, then he pressed his lips against her lower stomach. "Do you have a condom?"

She nodded. "I do. In the drawer of the bedside table."

He found the box, which was unopened, and removed one of the foil packets.

"Let me do it," she said, scooting to the edge of the bed.

"Please. Be my guest." He handed it over, standing before her, the tension in his hips and groin almost impossible to take.

She wrapped her fingers around his length and stroked firmly, looking up at him, her gaze locked on his. Heat didn't merely plume in his belly, it roared, spreading to his hips and down his thighs. He couldn't imagine her doing anything more pleasing, but then she switched to a lighter touch, her delicate fingers slow and teasing, and that made his need for her even deeper. He wasn't sure how many more passes he could take, but she finally rolled on the condom and he gathered himself.

He lowered his head, cupped the side of her face, and drew her into a deep kiss. He wanted to drink in her very being, and it felt as if she was doing the same to him, relishing every heavenly sensation of the other's touch. She eased herself to her back and he positioned himself at her entrance, driving inside. The moment was intense. As his heart thundered in his chest, he struggled to comprehend her warmth, and the way her body held on to him so tightly.

He went deeper and their bodies were fully joined. He inhaled her sweet scent and nestled his face in her neck while she wrapped her legs around him and muscled him closer with the backs of her calves. She tilted her hips with every stroke, meeting him when he was deepest. She seemed to want a faster pace, and so he made small but powerful thrusts, keeping their bodies as close as possible.

He was teetering on the edge of release, his breaths so shallow he couldn't fill his lungs. Hers were coming hard and fast, her lips parted and eyes closed as she seemed lost in the dreaminess of pleasure. He wanted those lips on his when she gave way. He wanted to feel every second of her vulnerability.

She gasped and clutched at the sheets. He realized just how close she was to release. "Kiss me," he said. He lowered his head and she raised hers, the kiss reckless and perfect. She bucked her hips against him and he thrust deeper, closing his eyes to feel just how tightly wound she was around him. He couldn't take much more, but he would do his damnedest to wait for her. With a sudden shock, she knocked back her head and arched her spine, and that was his cue to give in to the pleasure. He wasn't sure which way was up and which was down. His head spun fast and hard. Then he went into free fall, floating down to earth in a haze of deep satisfaction.

He collapsed next to her and she instantly curled into him. Their breaths slowed, falling into synchrony. She caressed the side of his face, sweetly rubbing her nose against his cheek and chin. Their lips connected, soft and warm, and he could feel the smile in her kiss. He couldn't think of another place he wanted to be. And he couldn't believe that it had taken him days to think about whether or not Astrid might be a good idea. She was better than that. She might be the miracle he hadn't known he was waiting for.

He dared to look at the clock. "We have twenty-five minutes before your guests arrive."

She groaned adorably and propped herself up on her elbow, dragging her fingers through his chest hair. "Whose idea was it to have a party anyway?"

He pressed a quick kiss to her lips. "I think it was yours." He didn't want to move a muscle, but he knew that the sooner he resigned himself to their social obligation for the evening, the better. "Come on. I think we'll live."

They both climbed off the bed and he padded into the bathroom to dispose of the condom. After washing his hands, he found his clothes and attempted to shake out the wrinkles that might be difficult to explain, especially to his sister, who did not miss many things. Not that he cared much at this point.

Astrid was in her closet as soon as he was dressed.

She was working her way into a pair of heels, sexy, mussed hair cascading past her shoulders. He couldn't resist the chance to step behind her, grasp her shoulders and kiss her on the cheek.

"Does this look okay?" she asked, turning to face him.

"You would look good in a paper bag, but yes. You look amazing." He kissed her on the lips. "I wish I could stay over, but I stupidly told the babysitter that I would be home before midnight." As soon as the words had left his lips, he realized the presumption he was making. "I mean, not that you were inviting me or anything."

She laughed quietly and grabbed a pair of earrings from a large drawer of jewelry. "I would love for you to stay, but I understand. Plus, I think that you and I would do well to take things slowly." She gestured with a nod to her bedroom. "That was amazing, and I can see how it could quickly become addictive, but you and I will need to rebuild some trust."

"Trust is immensely important."

"Good. Now let's go get ready for everyone to arrive."

They started in the kitchen, Clay in charge of setting up the bar while Astrid preheated the oven to pop in some appetizers. It'd been a long time since he'd done something so domestic like this with a woman other than his sister, and he was pleased to realize that this wasn't putting him on edge. Astrid's comment about rebuilding trust had done so much to reassure him that opening himself up to her might be the best decision he'd made in a long time.

Promptly at six thirty, Tara, and Grant arrived, followed shortly by Miranda's best friends from her office, Brittney and Shay. Clay was busy serving drinks when Miranda showed up. He dropped his party duty to help her with her coat.

"You told me this started at five," he muttered, kissing her on the cheek.

"Did I? That's weird. I guess it's just pregnancy brain. That's a thing, you know." Miranda was an expert at covering her tracks, but Clay could see through it by now. Apparently she really did want him to give Astrid a chance.

"Come on," he said. "Astrid bought all sorts of pregnancy-approved drinks."

Everyone congregated in the living room of Astrid's apartment while she and Clay shuttled out food. This was the exact right size for a party as far as Clay was concerned, and he also liked that everyone was so focused on discussing the baby. He knew very well that Miranda would have a big hill to climb as a single parent. A support system would be a big help. He hadn't allowed himself anyone's help with Delia, aside from Miranda's. He knew his sister wouldn't be so foolish.

"Any wagers on whether it's going to be a boy or a girl?" Grant asked, holding hands with Tara on the couch.

"I think girl," Tara answered.

Grant shook his head. "No way. It's a boy."

"We will find out soon enough," Astrid said. "But first, I have a gift for Miranda."

"Astrid," Miranda pled. "We said no gifts tonight."

Astrid shrugged it off playfully. "I'm not good at following the rules. We'll be right back." She waved Clay in the direction of her bedroom. Together, they picked up the stroller and carried it into the living room. Of course, the instant everyone saw it, there was an roar of laughter. The wrapping job had done its job.

"I wonder what this could be," Miranda joked, getting up from her seat.

Astrid was positively beaming. She took such joy in pleasing others. He wanted to kick himself for ever trying to shut that out. "Open it."

Miranda tore back some of the paper. "I can't believe you bought me the exact model of stroller I wanted. I mentioned it one time, totally in passing. How did you remember?"

Astrid tapped her temple with her finger. "It's all locked away up here."

Clay and everyone else watched as Astrid and Miranda embraced. It was a very sweet moment. Johnathon Sterling had certainly had magnificent taste in women. "Does this mean we get cupcakes?" he asked.

"Yes," Miranda said. "I'm dying to find out."

Clay brought out the platter of bakery treats

topped with white icing and a mix of pink and blue sprinkles. Astrid handed out dessert plates and napkins while everyone took a cupcake. "We'll count to three and everyone take a bite," Astrid said. "The frosting inside will give us our answer."

"Everyone ready?" Miranda asked. "One, two, three."

On cue, they followed the directive, which was quickly followed by a chorus of exclamations. *It's a girl.*

Miranda instantly burst into happy tears, as did Astrid. Clay found his eyes getting misty, but more than anything he was just so glad for his sister. She'd been through so much. These glimmers of joy were well-deserved. He quickly pulled her into a big embrace, rocking her back and forth in his arms.

"Just what you needed," Miranda said. "Another woman in your life."

"Are you kidding me? I'm the luckiest guy in the world." It was then that he caught sight of Astrid and she returned his gaze. Her smile lit up her entire face, especially her mesmerizing eyes. It was the truth. He was lucky. And this time, he was going to do his damnedest not to ruin it.

Eleven

The party at Astrid's ushered in two blissful weeks for Clay and Astrid—stolen kisses at work, lunch hours where they raced to Astrid's to be alone, sexy glances and flirtation in the stressful throes of finishing the second Seaport Promenade proposal. Every day was full of promise. Clay had a spring in his step he hadn't had in so long. He had optimism he wasn't sure he'd ever had. Astrid was amazing.

But he knew he had to make a change. They were also sneaking around. He might not be ready for full-blown commitment, and Astrid was clear about taking things slow, but it still didn't sit right with him. She'd been waiting for her happy ending for her whole life. He knew she deserved better.

For now, he had more pressing matters, namely Delia and her Halloween costume. Despite his best efforts over the months, Clay was not getting better at braids.

"Daddy, that looks bad." Delia frowned at him via her reflection in the mirror. "It doesn't look like the picture." She pointed at the cover of her *Snow Princess* DVD.

Indeed, he had failed to create six equal-sized braids circling her head, as well as the spirals that were supposed to be secured to her head with bobby pins. This hairstyle was like Princess Leia ran headlong into a Rubik's Cube, and he had zero confidence in his ability to solve the puzzle in time for trick-or-treating. As if the universe was conspiring against him, one of the elastics popped off its braid and it began to unravel. A single tear rolled down Delia's cheek, her lower lip quivered, and her chin dimpled.

"Please don't cry. I'm begging you. Don't cry."

"Then fix it," she pleaded.

That was it. He had to call in the big guns. "What if I call Astrid?"

"Yes, Daddy. Do it now."

He grabbed his cell phone from the bathroom counter and found Astrid on his favorites list.

"Hi," Astrid answered with a purr. One word and his stomach flipped. Memories of being with her over the last few weeks inundated his mind—blinding passion, unbelievable heat, and tender moments he never expected.

"I need help with Delia's hair for her Halloween costume. I have no idea what I'm doing and it'll be dark in an hour."

"I'm on my way. Fifteen minutes if I hit the lights right."

"Thank you."

"Of course. Anything for you."

Again he was struck by his luck. He couldn't mess this up. "Astrid will be here very soon, okay?" he asked Delia. "She'll fix everything."

Delia sat straighter, the tears a distant thought. "I'm excited to see her."

Clay felt a distinct tug in the vicinity of his heart. Every fiber of his being wanted Delia to like Astrid. There was so much riding on it, but he also knew that he couldn't force it. He had to let this happen naturally. "Good, honey. I'm glad."

Delia read a book while they waited for Astrid to arrive. Clay kept looking out the window, anxiously waiting. When her little silver convertible pulled into the driveway, he opened the door. "Thank you so much," he called as he thundered down the front stairs.

"Of course. I would never leave Delia in the lurch." Astrid climbed out of her car, looking amazing in a simple white blouse and curve-hugging blue jeans.

He pulled her into his arms and kissed her softly, but kept it quick. He wasn't ready for Delia to see that. "I'm glad you're here."

"So am I." She smiled wide. "Now let's fix Delia's hair."

Clay led her upstairs, through his master bedroom and into his bath, where Delia was still perched on a barstool, patiently waiting. "Astrid's here," he said.

Delia's eyes immediately lit up. "Thank you thank you thank you." It came out so fast, it was nearly a single word.

"I heard Daddy was having a hard time." Astrid set down her handbag on the marble counter and took one of Delia's hands.

"He was trying his hardest."

"I'm sure he was."

Astrid grinned. Then her gaze connected with Clay's. It felt like a lightning bolt straight through his heart. Witnessing this sweet exchange between her and Delia was making the effect even more powerful.

Clay stood and observed while Astrid went to work, sectioning Delia's hair and braiding thin strands, and picking up more hair as she went. He'd watched a few tutorial videos, but she made it look so effortless. By the time she had two of the six done, Clay felt like he could breathe again. It was going to look beautiful and Delia would be happy.

"How did you ever practice this?" he asked. "I thought you only had brothers."

Astrid wound a rubber band on the end of another braid. "I had a neighbor who watched me after school. She let me practice on her hair. My brothers were always busy with sports and both of my parents worked."

"I wish I had a brother," Delia said. "Or a sister. It's just me and Daddy and it gets very boring sometimes."

Astrid cleared her throat and shot Clay a look. "Well, brothers can be a big pain in the butt, too. So they're both good and bad." She juggled the strands of hair between her fingers. "You must have lots of friends at school to play with. Friends can be even better than siblings."

"I guess," Delia said.

Astrid finished the last braid. "I'll coil the ends and pin them, then lock them down with hairspray." She slid Clay a questioning look. "You do have hairspray, don't you?"

"I didn't realize it was that important."

Astrid dug through her purse. "Don't worry. I don't go anywhere without it." She returned to Delia's hair, making quick work of the final steps. "Well? Good?"

Delia picked up the DVD case and consulted it, then admired herself in the mirror. "It looks just like the picture." She hopped off the barstool and flung her arms around Astrid's waist. "Thank you so much."

This was a sight Clay hadn't been fully prepared for. Seeing Delia and Astrid forge a bond made his chest swell with pride and happiness.

"Can I put my costume on now?" Delia asked him.

"Yes. Do you need help?"

Delia shook her head. "I can do it."

"Just yell if you change your mind." Delia left and

Clay turned his sights to Astrid, who was leaning against the bathroom counter. Dammit, he wanted to kiss her more than almost anything. "You really bailed me out. It kills me when she's not happy."

"Of course it does. You're a great dad." She straightened and looked around the room, then walked off through the bathroom door and into his room. "So this is your bedroom. It's beautiful. Not overly masculine. Just the right amount."

Clay swallowed hard as he watched her walk over to the bed and swish her hand across the comforter. "Miranda designed it for me."

"Did you and your wife live here?"

"No. I was worried it would traumatize Delia to stay. I lucked out with this house, actually. I designed it for a client, but the whole time I was working on it, I was falling in love with it. The client ended up taking a job in Dubai and sold it to me."

"You did luck out."

"And we're so much closer to Miranda here. I knew I was going to need her help as much as possible."

"But you didn't call her about the braids?"

That was when it hit him—his first thought had been to seek Astrid's help. He was so conditioned to go to Miranda. Apparently that had changed. "You offered. And I figured I needed an expert."

Astrid nodded in agreement, but something in the look on her face said that she was on to him. If she hadn't known that he was falling for her, perhaps she knew it now. "I do know my Nordic hairstyles."

"I'd better make sure she doesn't need help with her costume."

"Yes. Go. I'll wait downstairs. Or maybe I should go. I know you two have a big night ahead of you."

"No. Please stay." He hoped she understood that he meant for her to stay over.

"Overnight?"

"Yes."

"But Delia. I appreciate you asking for my help. I do. But this is the first time I've seen your bedroom, and we've had a whole bunch of sex over the last two weeks. It's clear that you're still not sure about folding me into this part of your life and I understand. I was the one who said we should take it slow. I don't want to intrude."

"You aren't intruding. I want you here. This is long overdue and I'm sorry for that." He pulled her into his arms and kissed her tenderly, hoping he could convey just how much he meant that.

"It's okay, Clay. You don't need to apologize. We're both figuring this out as we go."

He wanted her to stay. He was letting down the wall.

She reached for his arm and rubbed it gently. The connection between them was familiar and strong. "Check on Delia. I'll be downstairs."

"Perfect."

Clay disappeared through the doorway and Astrid took her time meandering down the upstairs hall, admiring the handful of framed photographs of Clay and Delia. They had the same hair color, but not quite the same features. Astrid wondered if she looked like her mother, if Clay had to see his ex-wife in his sweet daughter.

She continued to the landing, which was open on both sides and overlooked the living room below. Soft strains of late-day sunshine streamed in through tall, skinny windows that looked like matchsticks, artfully arranged on the stairwell wall. Every space Clay created was aesthetically perfect and designed with purpose, a harmonious joining of form and function. Even with the home's seemingly simple modern design, she knew the care and love that had gone into planning it. Warm wood tones, the way the eye was drawn from one space to the next, and the central role of natural light in every room mirrored the true heart and spirit of its creator.

She wandered into his showpiece of a kitchen, just off the living room, and helped herself to a glass of water from the massive double fridge. On the counter was a large bowl of Halloween candy. She couldn't help but smile at the thought of Clay shopping for bags of chocolate bars and peanut butter cups with Delia. Why did everything he did have to be so beguiling?

"Here comes the Snow Princess!" Delia called from upstairs.

Astrid hustled out into the hall in time to see the little girl carefully descending the stairs in her icy-blue-and-silver princess gown. Clay followed behind her, beaming with pride.

"How pretty do I look?" Delia asked, twirling in a circle at the bottom of the stairs.

"You're the prettiest ever. You look exactly like the Snow Princess."

Delia turned to her dad. "Can we go yet?"

"Sure. I just want to talk to Astrid for a minute if that's okay."

"I'll go find my trick-or-treat bag." Delia skittered off.

"Do you want to come with us?" Clay asked.

Astrid did like the idea of being included, but they'd had a breakthrough upstairs and she didn't want to push it. She would have time with Delia. Tonight was all about daddy and daughter. "I would love to, but who's going to hand out the candy?"

"I put the bowl on a chair outside my gate and let the kids grab whatever they want."

Astrid saw the perfect compromise. "Why don't you and Delia trick-or-treat, and I'll take candy duty. I'll be here when you get back."

"Are you sure?"

"This is a special time for you two. She'll only be five once."

He took Astrid's hand, tugging her close, making her light-headed with a kiss that grazed her mouth. "You promise you'll still be here?"

"I'm not going anywhere."

Clay took a few dozen photos of Delia. Then the two marched off down the driveway and through the gate. Astrid decided to bring a chair out to the sidewalk and hand out candy there. She'd get more takers that way. The night air was chilly, but not unbearably so with the light sweater she'd brought. Groups of children streamed past her, dressed as superheroes and witches, princesses and cartoon characters. Astrid loved handing out the candy and speaking to the little ones as their eager faces lit up with excitement at a new treat in their bag. She could often go for days at a time now not thinking about how badly she wanted to become a mom, but on a day like today, that yearning within her had new life.

She worked very hard to stay positive about it. She would become a mother one day, by adoption if necessary. The task before that was finding love. The feelings that were blooming between her and Clay were sure starting to feel like that, but she was in no rush to put a label on anything. They both had their reasons for being wary. Still, she took the phone call about the braid disaster as a good sign. She'd been his first thought. There'd been a time when she wasn't sure she'd even been his last.

An hour and a half later, Clay and Delia returned. They both smiled as Delia held up the enormous bag of loot she'd raked in.

"All done?" Astrid asked.

"I don't think it's possible for her to carry any

more candy." Clay glanced at the empty bowl. "Is it seriously all gone?" He sounded more than a little sad.

She showed him the contents of her sweater pocket—a handful of assorted chocolate bars. "I had a feeling you'd want your own supply."

"You know my sweet tooth better than anyone." He reached for her hand. "Let's go in and put Delia to bed, then open a bottle of wine."

A little thrill wound its way down Astrid's spine. "That sounds wonderful."

The three walked inside. Delia protested when Clay took her bag of candy. "Daddy. That's mine."

"I know. And you can have it tomorrow. You've had more than enough for tonight."

"Don't steal any." To drive her point home, Delia scolded him with her finger.

"I won't. I promise. Why don't you go upstairs and put on your pj's?"

"Can Astrid help me?"

An instant of inner conflict crossed Clay's face, but just as fast, it evaporated. "Sure. I'll be up in a minute to tuck you in."

Astrid felt honored by Delia's request, and went upstairs with her, helping her change into her pajamas and get ready for bed. She tried to ignore the way the littlest of things, like watching as she brushed her teeth, felt so right. Oddly enough, it helped her see why Clay had worried so much about Delia getting attached to her. Astrid was more attached to them both with each passing second. "Do you want me to take out your braids?" Astrid asked.

"No. I want to wear them to school tomorrow." Delia rubbed her tired eyes as Clay appeared in the doorway.

"Good night, Delia," Astrid said from the doorway. She watched Clay tuck his daughter in, admiring him in profile as he leaned down to kiss her on the cheek. Astrid's heart was practically melting into a puddle on the floor.

He took her hand and they tiptoed back downstairs to the kitchen. Clay opened that promised bottle of wine and poured them each a glass. Astrid traded him a candy bar from her sweater pocket. Amusement flickered in his eyes.

"You totally have my number," he said, then popped it into his mouth.

"Do I?" She still wasn't sure.

He cupped the side of her head with his hand, rubbing his thumb back and forth over her cheek, sending her heart racing. "You do. You were such a lifesaver tonight."

"It was just some braids. I was happy to do it."

"It's more than that. You didn't hesitate to drop everything, jump in your car and get over here."

She leaned into his warmth as he pressed her against the kitchen counter, and she gazed up into his eyes. "I'd do anything for you or Delia. I care about you both deeply." It was liberating to come out with the truth.

"I care about you, too. So much." He kissed her softly, his tongue tracing the contour of her lower lip. "I want you to stay tonight."

She wanted so badly to accept the invitation. His kisses and touch were everything…it would be so easy to say yes and ask him to take her upstairs. But she had to be sure he was thinking about what he was saying. She had to be sure this was real. "But Delia. I don't want you to forget about the things you've tried so hard to protect. Your daughter. And your heart." She smoothed her hand across his chest. "Those are not unimportant things."

He pulled his head back, contemplative and even a bit brooding, showing her shades of the conflicted man he was when they first met. "I know. You're right, they are important." His eyes shifted to an even darker hue. The color had to be reflecting at least some of the struggle inside him.

"So take a minute to think about what tomorrow morning might be like when she wakes up and sees me in the house. Think about what you will say. If we cross that bridge, there's no going back." She sucked in a gulp of air, wondering if her inner conflict came close to matching his. "It's okay if you tell me you're not ready. But it's not okay for you to tell me tomorrow that you want to return to sneaking around the office or meeting up at my place. I don't want to force you into anything, but I do think I deserve that much." She held her breath, not knowing how he was going to take the ultimatum. She'd suggested they take things slow, but she'd never meant for them to go backwards. She needed forward movement in her life now.

"You deserve more than that. So much more."

What was he saying? Was he about to make his old argument about how he couldn't give her what she wanted and needed? "What does that mean, Clay?"

Without warning, he swept her up into his arms. He looked her right in the eye, his eyes full of promises. Astrid's heart was beating so fiercely she could feel it from her head to her toes. "It means that I'm all in."

Twelve

Clay called Miranda on Monday morning as he was driving into work. "How's the best sister in the world?" he asked over speakerphone.

"Excuse me? Who is this?"

"Oh, come on. You know who it is."

Miranda tittered on the other end of the phone. "I know what the caller ID says, but you don't sound at all like yourself."

He sucked in a deep breath, preparing to send this bit of news out into the world. "I'm in love."

Miranda gasped. "No!"

"It's the truth." Having made his confession, he told Miranda all about the weekend with Astrid staying over at the house. He told her how it had put all remaining shreds of worry to rest. Astrid did more than fit perfectly into his life with Delia, she made it better. He loved seeing the two of them together, talking, laughing and having fun. Beyond that, the moments when it was just the two of them were pure magic. Astrid made everyone around her happier, especially him.

"Oh, my God. I am so happy to hear this. What did she say when you told her?"

He hadn't yet admitted his feelings to Astrid, but he'd said it to himself several times over the course of the weekend. It initially came as a surprise, but it had ultimately come naturally, which was exactly what he'd hoped for. He hadn't pushed it. It made sense to both his heart and his logical brain. "I haven't told her. Not yet. I need to find the right time." He also had to decide what went along with those three little words. A ring? An invitation to move in? She'd wanted to take things slow, but right now, he wanted to step on the gas.

"Clay, I have been waiting to hear this for what feels like forever. I'm ridiculously happy."

He pulled his car into the parking garage at Sterling Enterprises. "Well, good. I'm super happy, too."

"I have to go check my email and get into the office, but let's talk later, okay?"

"Sounds like a plan." Clay climbed out of his car. He strode into the building and hopped on the elevator, fighting back an irrational desire to whistle. He was not the sort of guy who did that. The doors slid open when he reached the Sterling offices. "Good morning," he said to Roz, the receptionist, stopping at her desk.

Roz peered up at him, bewildered. "Good morning, Mr. Morgan. Can I help you with something?"

"No. I just realized that I rarely take the time to thank you for everything you do to make the office run so smoothly."

"Thank you. It's nice to hear you say that."

He started off down the hall, realizing he'd nearly forgotten what it was like to be this happy. For the first time in a very long time, he not only felt as though he had a glimpse of a brighter future, he had a clear view of it. "Good morning," he said to Tara when he spotted her marching out of her office.

"Have you talked to Astrid?" The edge of annoyance in her voice was a jarring contrast to his mood. "I tried to call her, but she's not answering her phone."

Clay cleared his throat. He hadn't merely talked to Astrid that morning. They'd made love, and it had been spectacular. It partly explained his giddiness. "She's not in the office yet, but I'm sure she'll be here very soon." As far as he knew, she was at her apartment getting ready for work.

"We have a problem. That revised deadline she gave us for the Seaport presentation? It doesn't exist. They didn't move the date back. They moved it up. It's Wednesday."

Clay's merriment evaporated. Just like that. "Wait. What? That's in two days. We thought we had *ten*."

Clay's thoughts flew to the calendar and his to-do list. There was no way they would catch up and finish everything by Friday. It would require all-nighters, and even then, it might not be enough. How had it happened again that they had a last-minute panic situation on the Seaport project? "That has to be a mistake. Astrid wouldn't get that wrong."

"I got a reminder email from the city, so I called and asked to speak to Sandy. There is no Sandy working in the city planner's office."

None of this was adding up. At all. From the depths of his pocket, Clay's cell rang. "Maybe this is her. Hold on." He fished it out of his pocket. "It's Miranda. That's weird. I just talked to her." He sent the call to voice mail.

"Take it if you want. I need to update Grant. It's all hands on deck. Let's meet in an hour. And help me find Astrid."

Clay sent Miranda a text. Was that a butt dial? We have a crisis in the office. Talk to you later? His phone rang. It was Miranda. Again. "What's up?"

"I have my own crisis." Her voice was teeming with panic.

"What happened? We were just on the phone ten minutes ago."

"I need to talk to Astrid right now and I can't reach her on her cell phone or her office line."

What in the hell was going on? "Wait. Why do you need to call Astrid? You aren't going to tell her what we talked about, are you?"

"No. That's not why I need to talk to her. I can't tell you. You'll freak out."

Now he was flat-out worried. "Please tell me what's going on."

"No. I need to hear it from her. I need to know if it's true. I just got an email." Her voice cracked. "I don't know how to say this. It says it's from Johnathon."

Clay hadn't been stunned many times in his life, but that was the only word that fit this moment. "That's not possible." Clay didn't want to state the obvious, but it had to be said. His sister must be confused. "He's dead."

"I realize that, Clay. The man was my husband. I was with him when he died. Hence, my panic at receiving an email from him, especially one that says the things this one does."

"You have to forward it to me right now. If it's making you upset and it has to do with Astrid, you have to share it with me."

"No. Clay. This will hurt you, too, if you read it."

He failed to see how that was possible. "You think I care about that? You are my sister. I am always here for you. Always. Please send me the email. I promise that whatever's in it, I will take it all in stride." *Things today can't get any worse. Or any more strange.*

A heavy sigh came from the other end of the line. "Okay. Sent. It has to be a hoax. Some cruel prank."

The number on Clay's inbox ticked one higher.

There was the mysterious message, with the original sender listed as Johnathon Sterling. Even more astounding, it was from his Sterling Enterprises email account. Clay clicked on it and began to read, but when he hit the second sentence, it was like running right into a brick wall.

Dear Miranda,
I need to tell you something that will upset you, but the truth needs to come out. Astrid and I continued our relationship after we were divorced. The last time I made love to her was after you and I were engaged. She has a way of drawing a man in and convincing him she is perfect. Obviously I fell for it more than once. I hope you can forgive me.
Johnathon

Clay had a lot of conflicting thoughts vying for his attention, but the one that came through loudest was that there was no way this could be true. The source, a dead man, certainly called the validity into question. Clay expanded the message header, and the servers all checked out. This had come from a Sterling Enterprises email account. On a very long list of things he needed to do today, he would have to reach out to the company's IT department and see if they could help him solve the mystery.

"Clay? Are you there?" Miranda asked.

"Yeah. Sorry. Let me see what I can figure out about this, okay? This has to be fake. I don't know who would send this, but I'll find out. I'll find Astrid. It will all be fine. I don't want you to worry."

"I feel so helpless and confused right now." Miranda's anguished tone made him want to reach through the phone and hug her. The thought of anyone hurting her put him in an extremely protective frame of mind, but he was sure this bizarre story wouldn't turn out to be true.

"I'll get to the bottom of this. I swear."

"Call me as soon as you know something," Miranda said. "I love you."

"Love you, too."

Clay hung up and took a moment to shut his eyes and breathe. None of this could be real. There had to be a logical explanation. Still, he couldn't keep thoughts of the last few days, weeks, and months with Astrid from shuffling through his mind. He'd fought so hard at first to keep her away, all to protect himself and his daughter. Had he let a beautiful face cloud his judgment again?

That's not it. That can't be it. Everything you feel for her is real. You have to find out the truth.

He tried Astrid's cell, but it went straight to her voice mail. Clay paced in his office, feeling like a caged animal. He was desperate for Astrid to arrive. All he needed was to see her face and hear her say that this obviously crazy story was a lie.

Luckily, he didn't have to wait long. "You were looking for me?" Astrid appeared in his doorway, holding a bakery bag, fresh-faced and gorgeous. The sight of her smoothed his ragged edges. "I stopped to get you a doughnut."

"That's so sweet." He rushed to her and kissed her cheek. This was no time for sweets, but he was thankful nonetheless. "I've been trying to reach you. Tara has, too."

"What? I didn't get any calls." She dug her phone out of her handbag, her eyes wide with surprise. "I take that back. You did call me. So did Miranda and Tara. I turned the ringer off when I was at your house all weekend and I forgot to turn it back on. What's going on?"

Clay quietly closed the door behind her so they could have some privacy. This could be an awkward conversation and he wanted to protect her from office gossip. "We have two big problems. I think you should sit."

"What in the world? You're scaring me." As he suggested, she perched in one of the chairs opposite his desk.

He took the seat next to her. "The first thing is Seaport. There is no deadline extension. It's this Wednesday."

Astrid reared back her head and her luscious mouth formed a pout. "No. That can't be right. I'll call Sandy and get it straightened out."

"Tara called the city and she doesn't work there, Astrid. They're saying she never did."

"I have her cell number. I can call her directly."

"You should probably do that, but I don't know what good it's going to do. That doesn't change the fact that we had the wrong date, and now we have the right one." Clay was hit with a truly abhorrent thought. What if Astrid was lying? Was she capable? He hated that he was even thinking it—it clawed at his insides—but he couldn't help the way his brain was wired. Skepticism and doubt had long been his default. *Take a breath. She would never lie.*

"I'll call her as soon as you tell me what else is wrong."

This part was going to be treacherous. He didn't relish it at all. The pain of losing Johnathon was still fresh for everyone, but especially the wives. He'd heard it well up in his sister mere minutes ago. "Miranda received an email. As outlandish as this might sound, it not only came from Johnathon's Sterling account, the message itself was written as though it was from him. It says that you and he were romantically involved after your divorce." Every new word out of his mouth made this sound more impossible, but that wasn't as much comfort as he would've liked. He couldn't get past this feeling that something was very, very wrong. "It says that you two slept together after he and Miranda got engaged."

He watched as the color drained from Astrid's face and her expression fell. Her beautiful facade crumbled. More telling, she offered no defense. He felt like the rug had been pulled out from under him. *Oh, my God. Is it really true?*

Astrid was sure she was going to be sick. Her stomach pitched. Her head spun. She wanted to curl into a ball, shut her eyes and make this all go away. But the time had come. The day she'd feared so much was here. She wanted to believe that he would understand, but she was so unsure. Everything between them was still so fragile and new.

Craving the comfort of his touch, she reached for his hand, but he didn't curl his fingers around hers as he normally would. His skin felt cold. In many ways, it felt as if he already knew the truth and had passed judgment. "Let me explain."

His cheeks colored with what she feared might be anger. "Is it true?"

Tell him and get it over with. "It is." The confession brought no relief. He dropped her hand. She could see the toll this was taking on him. She'd known all along that this would happen. That was why she'd tried so hard to shoulder the burden on her own.

"I can't even believe what you're saying. Why did you do that? When he was about to marry someone else?"

"It was an accident."

Impatient and exasperated, he stormed up out of his chair and crossed the room, deepening the sense of divide between them. "You realize how ridiculous that sounds, right?"

"I had no idea he was romantically involved with someone else. I was tucked away at home in Norway. When we divorced, I lost so many friends. I didn't know what he was up to here at home."

"Even if that's true, you kept this from my sister? After you two have gotten so close?" He ran his hands through his hair, his eyes wild with anguish. "Is that why you bought her that stroller? Threw her the party? Out of guilt?"

Astrid knew she was in the wrong here, but that was deeply hurtful. "If it's true? I wouldn't lie about this."

"Oh, but you did. You hid this from Miranda. You hid it from me, the whole time we were together. You had plenty of opportunities to tell me. I'm looking back at every moment we had together and now I have to see it through a lens of lies."

Now she could see how doomed she and Clay had been from the start. She could have told Miranda the day she found out and dealt with the repercussions, but that only would have given him more ammunition for his argument that they didn't work well together. "Please don't look at what we have that way. There were no lies. There was this one thing that I kept to myself."

"And I don't see how you could do that."

"I knew it was just going to hurt everyone. When I arrived at Johnathon's funeral, I knew nothing of Miranda or their marriage. You can ask Tara or Grant. He kept me in the dark. I don't know why he did that." It was yet another mystery of Johnathon that might never be solved.

"The email makes it sound like you seduced him, not the other way around."

"I don't understand that part of what you said. Who would pose as Johnathon and send an email?"

"I don't know, Astrid. None of today makes sense. Why would Sandy appear out of nowhere a few weeks ago and give you the wrong information about Seaport?"

The wheels in Astrid's head were turning…her run-in with Sandy and how all of this might be connected. "That's it. That has to be it. Johnathon's brother. I think there's some connection between Sandy and him." Her mind flew to the first time she met Clay, right in this office. She was not only instantly attracted to him, she was equally intrigued by his quiet intensity.

She walked over to the photo on his credenza, the one of Johnathon and Miranda on their wedding day, flanked by Clay and Delia. She picked it up and showed it to him. "The day I met you, I saw this photo, and that was when it clicked. Remember, I asked when the wedding was? That's why I rushed out into the hall that day. I'm sure you thought I was crazy, but I was in shock." She looked back up at him, realizing this bit of information wasn't convincing him that she was telling the truth. "I told Tara right after that. I think Sandy was out in the hall."

The incredulous look on his face told her all she needed to know. He didn't believe her. "This all feels like you covering your tracks. How am I supposed to trust you now?"

That felt like a dagger aimed straight at her heart. She wanted to defend herself, but even more important, she wanted to say something that would make Clay take a deep breath, step back, and look objectively at what was going on. He was letting his old fears and distrust cloud his judgment. "You can trust me because I love you."

He turned to her and froze, but didn't say a thing. His expression was calculating, his eyes reflecting the complicated processes that went through his head. It was part of parcel of Clay, and such a huge component of what she loved about him. But in that moment, it was the most devastating thing she'd ever endured. Love wasn't a conclusion to arrive at. It was either in your heart or it wasn't. Clearly, he didn't feel the way she did.

She stepped closer to him, aching to be wrapped up in his embrace, but he crossed his arms to keep her out. It was like she was watching him rebuild that old familiar wall around himself, stacking it up, brick by brick. "You really don't believe me, do you?"

"No matter what facts come out, Astrid, there is one set of details that isn't in dispute. You knew I had trust issues. You knew I had very strong reasons to protect myself and Delia and how badly we'd been hurt." His voice was a vessel for his pain, cracked in two. "And you let me let you in, even when you were carrying around a secret that you knew would hurt Miranda. She is the one person who has always been by my side and she's going to be destroyed when she finds out this is true."

"I'm sorry, Clay. I truly am. I will make things right with Miranda. I'll explain it all."

He shook his head emphatically, his jaw tight and his eyes dark. "No. I can't let you do that. It's over, Astrid. There is no more you and me. I can't let you be close to me anymore."

"Just like that? Even when I love you?" Once again, her opening of her heart and soul went unanswered.

There was a knock at the door, which Clay quickly took as his excuse to end their conversation. Tara poked her head in. "Astrid, what happened with the Seaport deadline?"

This was officially the worst day ever. Not only was everyone mad at her, Clay had just ripped her heart out. "Let me try to track down Sandy. Something sketchy is going on."

Tara and Clay exchanged glances. "It doesn't matter at this point," Tara said. "That won't change the deadline. The other firms are going to be ready to present on Wednesday and we have to be, too. Grant is in the conference room. We need to sit down and figure out a strategy. Right now."

Astrid and Clay dutifully followed Tara down the hall, but Astrid felt as though she was about to find her head on the chopping block. She'd stupidly allowed herself to think that she could find new purpose at Sterling. Clearly, she'd managed to ruin what chance she had, and the thought of trying to salvage it was so daunting. All paths at Sterling led to Clay. There was no avoiding him, which had been the trouble all along.

Inside the meeting room, several junior architects and members of the support staff were assembled. Grant stood at the large whiteboard, where he'd written up a flow chart of the things that needed to happen before Wednesday. It was so much work. An absolute mountain of it, and it was all her fault that they had to rush to complete it. Astrid sat at the table, next to Tara. Clay chose to stand on the other side of the room, leaning against the wall.

"Thank you, everyone, for dropping everything to help us save the Seaport project," Grant said. "There was a mistake with the deadline we were working under, and we have an enormous amount of work to finish by Wednesday morning." Grant took a drink of water from a glass on the table. Meanwhile, Astrid felt all eyes on her. If the staff hadn't expressly been told that it was her mistake, the Sterling Enterprises rumor mill had clearly kicked into high gear. "Clay and I will finish the final plans, along with help from the junior architects. Tara and Astrid will work from the administrative side to prepare the presentation and the materials that accompany that."

Tara rose from her seat. "We'll be working late the next two nights, and coming in early the next two mornings. But Grant and I want everyone to know just how much we appreciate your extraordinary effort. The Seaport Promenade project was a passion project for Johnathon Sterling, and it will be an important piece of his legacy if we land it. We have a good chance, but it's going to take all of us to make it happen. Now let's get to work."

The noise level went up as everyone broke into conversation and began to file out of the room. Astrid pulled Tara aside. As terrible as Astrid had felt when she walked into this meeting, it was now worse. If they lost the project, it would be Astrid's fault, and she would have let everyone down when all they were trying to do was honor Johnathon's life and career. "I don't even know what to say other than I'm sorry. I feel like that's so inadequate, though."

"We all make mistakes, Astrid. We'll get through it."

"I know. But it's really important to me to do a good job, and that means helping the team. Right now, I'm hurting us."

"Okay, then. Let's focus on doing the opposite."

Astrid received the message, loud and clear. "Okay. I'll stay overnight the next two nights if I need to."

"Good. Because that might be what we'll need."

Astrid ducked out of the conference room and immediately pulled up the contact information for Sandy on her phone. She called her cell, but it rang and rang. It didn't even go to voice mail. Astrid knew there was something that wasn't right about this, but she had nothing to go on. This phone number was the only piece of information she had about Sandy.

Astrid hurried to her office and gathered her Seaport materials, armfuls of binders and notebooks, and began carting them off to a second meeting room, where she and Tara could collaborate, along with a team of four admins. They worked straight through the day, having lunch and dinner brought in. Astrid made several more attempts at reaching Sandy, but had the same result every time—endless ringing and no answer. Another dead end.

Around 10:00 p.m., Tara sent the admins home and suggested she and Astrid go catch up with Clay and Grant. Astrid was a bundle of nerves walking down the hall, not knowing how Clay would receive her. Tara immediately went to Grant when they arrived, leaving Clay and Astrid to talk.

"Hey," she said. "How's it going for you guys?"

"Slow. Exhausting." Clay's voice was clipped and terse.

Astrid was tired, too, and his attitude toward her wasn't making any of this easier. "I tried to call Sandy. I don't get any answer. I guess she lied to me. I don't really understand it."

"I know you're trying to dig yourself out of this

hole, but I think you should probably accept where you are. I spoke to the IT department and they verified the email Miranda got came from Sterling. And since we both know that Sandy has no access to Sterling and hasn't worked here in nearly two months now, it seems to me like those two things are unrelated." He cast a glance at her, but quickly returned his sights to his work. "And it doesn't change anything. It doesn't change anything at all. Let me get back to work so I can get through these next two days, okay?"

Astrid pressed her lips together hard to ward off the tears stinging her eyes. She would not cry. She had to stay positive, even in the face of unimaginable obstacles. Everything she cared about had taken a hit today—her love for Clay, her relationship with Tara and Miranda, and the fate of Sterling Enterprises. These were also the things keeping her in San Diego. The only things.

Maybe the writing was on the wall. She'd wondered if she could build a life here, and she'd made a valiant effort. Perhaps it was time to admit defeat and return to Norway. She'd never last at Sterling beyond Wednesday if this was to be her working relationship with Clay. If she'd thought it had been strained at the beginning, this was so much worse. She loved him and she couldn't undo her feelings. She couldn't wish them away. But she also couldn't do a thing to change everything else that had happened.

She could only find a way to move forward. And it looked as though she would be doing that alone.

Thirteen

Wednesday morning had arrived. Astrid's second all-nighter at Sterling was done. She was exhausted and sad, especially as she wished Tara good luck on the presentation, which was only hours away. She didn't have the chance to say goodbye to Clay, as he was downstairs loading the Sterling Enterprises van, but she'd planned accordingly.

"You two will do great. I know it," Astrid said.

"You're sure about leaving?" Tara asked. "I think we salvaged the presentation, and I know people are giving you the cold shoulder now, but they'll come around. A few sleepless nights will eventually become a distant memory."

Astrid was sure of only one thing, which was that

this had been a fun experiment, but she'd become collateral damage. "The thing I loved about working here was being part of the team. That's gone now. For right now, this is the best choice for me."

"Did you tell Clay?"

Astrid held up a note. "I'll leave this on his desk. He can read it when he comes back."

Tara spread her arms wide, and they embraced. "Keep me posted on everything."

"You, too," Astrid said. "Let me know how the presentation goes."

They parted ways and Astrid dropped by Clay's office one last time. She didn't stay long or reminisce as she was apt to do. She couldn't afford to rehash what might have been. After two days of very little sleep, she was too exhausted. She'd done all she could do, and now she had work of a different sort to do. She had to pack.

The clothes she'd brought for Johnathon's funeral went into one of three suitcases, along with everything she'd bought since she arrived. She decided to leave the navy gown she'd worn for the Architect of the Year awards in a garment bag in the closet. That dress had wonderful memories. She hoped that one day she'd be able to look back at it fondly. Right now, it simply hurt too much.

When she was done, she pulled her final suitcase into her foyer. She took one more pass through her beloved apartment, making sure the fridge was empty and lights were turned off. She had someone to come by and water the plants. She would return. She just wasn't quite sure when. Perhaps when the hurt subsided.

Bright light streamed in through the one window that didn't have the shade drawn, California sun dancing on the glossy wood floor. It was hard to believe everything that had happened in the months since Johnathon had died. She'd come to San Diego thinking she was bidding farewell to her ex-husband. She'd never dreamed she was embarking on a whole new life, or that she might find love. She'd never imagined that it would all blow up in such spectacular fashion.

She'd forged a friendship with Tara and Miranda, who were the closest she'd ever come to having sisters. She'd found a new career path, one she believed she was quite good at, despite the missteps she had made. And most important, she'd had a glimpse of true love with Clay. It was still there in her heart, thumping away and reminding her of its presence, but she was resigned to the inevitability of it all. He wasn't able to let her all the way in. She couldn't blame him. She'd pushed his limits.

Astrid's phone beeped with a text. It was from Tara. Presentation went well. Thank you for all you did.

I'm so glad. It was the least I could do.

Leaving soon?

Astrid fought a tear. This was one of the hardest things she'd ever done, but it was the only thing that made sense. She needed time to think. She needed distance to figure out her next step. Yes. Flight departs in a few hours.

Safe travels.

The driver she'd hired arrived at her door and took her bags downstairs to the car.

"I'd like to make one stop before we go to the airport, please," she told him out on the street.

The driver consulted his watch. "Will we have time?"

"Yes. I won't be long." She gave him the address and sat back in the car, trying to remind herself that just like her decision to move to San Diego had been temporary, so could her return to Norway. She didn't have to stay anywhere. She could move to New York. Back to Los Angeles. Or perhaps somewhere else. Wherever it was, she was done with love. There would be no matching what she'd had with Clay. Maybe there would come a day when he could forgive her, if only so she could have some closure.

The driver pulled into Miranda's driveway and opened the door for Astrid.

"I'll just be a few minutes," she said, then marched up to ring the bell.

Miranda answered a minute later, looking surprised. "Astrid. What are you doing here?"

"I know you work from home on Wednesdays." Astrid handed over an envelope. "I wanted to give you this."

Miranda glanced at it, then looked out to the driveway, spotting the driver. "Do you want to come in?"

Astrid shook her head, not wanting to drag this out. "This will be quick. I know that you and I spoke about the Johnathon situation over the phone, but I wanted a chance to apologize in person. I never would have allowed that to happen if I'd known about your engagement. I hope you know me well enough by now to know that's true."

"I know. I do. I'm sorry I was so angry when we spoke about it on Monday. I was in shock."

"And I only kept it a secret because I knew there could never be a resolution. You can't confront Johnathon. You or I will never be able to find out why he did what he did." Astrid's sights fell to Miranda's belly. "More than anything, I didn't want to taint the image you have of the father of your child, especially when you're still grieving."

Miranda smiled. "I understand. I do." She looked down at the envelope. "What's in here?"

"I'd like to give my shares of Sterling to the baby. I don't see any point in me being there anymore. I've finished my work, and Tara and Clay did the presentation this morning. They'll find out before Christmas whether or not they landed the Seaport job."

"Astrid, no. Have you talked to Tara about this?"

Astrid nodded. "I did. She agreed that my presence at Sterling wasn't great for morale right now. But the real truth is that I can't work with Clay." It felt so funny to say that out loud, the very thing he'd always said about her. How things had changed. "There was always this part of him that couldn't let me in."

Miranda looked out at the car again. "Is there somewhere you have to be? I feel like we need to talk about this."

"Actually, I'm headed for the airport. I'm going back to Norway."

"What? No. You can't leave. Don't you want to be here when the baby is born?"

Astrid felt as if her heart was being torn out right now, but she didn't see how she could stay. Miranda and the baby were inextricably tied to Clay. "My parents are expecting me. And they'd like me to be there for Christmas."

"Okay. I understand." Miranda reached for Astrid's shoulder. "But I just want to say one thing. As the person who has been through the worst of the worst with my brother, I can tell you that when he closes himself off, he's protecting something. There have been many times when it was me. There have been many times when it was Delia. That's all it is. His defenses."

Astrid sighed. "I can't fault him for wanting to shield the people he loves." *It's a huge part of why I love him.*

"Maybe you two need to have one last conversation? He'll be here with Delia in a little bit. He decided to take a half day at work so he could spend some time unwinding."

This was why she had to leave San Diego. She couldn't live her life trying to dodge the man she loved, all because it would only dredge up pain. "I'm sorry, Miranda. But I have to go."

Clay left the presentation and headed back to Sterling Enterprises with very little sense of triumph, even when it had gone incredibly well. The problem was Astrid. She'd worked so hard to drag them over the finish line, and she hadn't been there to get any credit or do a victory lap. All of that was on him. He knew how much she struggled to work with him when he was pushing her away. He'd started their working relationship on that course. And he was still having a hard time steering off of it.

The trouble was that every magical memory of Astrid was colored by the pall of her secret. Now that he was a few days removed from the revelation, he was starting to dig down to what was really bothering him. He was terrified of being blinded by a woman. He was scared of being duped and having his whole life fall apart as a result. It had happened before, and everything had rushed back when he discovered Astrid's secret.

He arrived back at his office and planned to take care of a few minor things before leaving to pick up Delia from school. He'd made plans with Miranda to spend the afternoon relaxing out by the pool. It had been unseasonably warm for early November, and Miranda kept the water at a balmy 82 degrees, all to keep Delia happy. But that was when he spotted an envelope on his desk, with his name scrawled in Astrid's frenetic handwriting.

Dear Clay,

I hope the presentation went well today. If it was half as brilliant as you, it was a home run. I want to let you know that I am going back to Norway. I need to clear my head and think about what my future might hold. I plan to come back eventually, but as to when that will be, I don't know. I also don't know that I will stay.

I don't want you to think of me as a repeat of the hurt in your life. Yes, I'm leaving, but you will never have to guess why. It's not because I don't love you. It's because I do. And I know I've hurt you. I know that by proxy, this will hurt Delia. I'm doing everything I can to minimize the pain so you can heal. I want that for you more than anything.

I will never regret our time together. Even when we were at odds, I had hope that we would find our way through it. I know now that our timing was all wrong. I arrived when you weren't ready, and I pushed even though you told me so. You gave me an opening and

I took it, but only because I was desperate for
even a minute with you. I'm so thankful we
had more than that.
With all my love,
Astrid
P.S. Please kiss Delia for me. If she asks where
I went, tell her I've gone looking for the Snow
Princess. I'll bring her back if I track her down.

Perhaps it was the exhaustion, but Clay was struggling to understand what he'd just read. *She's leaving? She can't do that.* He had to stop her. Right now.

He flung his laptop bag over his shoulder and
jogged down the hall to the lobby. His first instinct
was to take the stairs, but the maintenance people
were painting them. *Dammit.* He pressed the elevator button and stared at the numbers, as if that might
possibly make it go faster. Finally it dinged and the
door slid open.

JJ from the tech department appeared out of nowhere. Clay had asked him to dig deeper on the email
that was supposedly from Johnathon. "Mr. Morgan.
We got an answer for you about that message. It
wasn't really from a Sterling server."

Clay stuck his arm out to hold the elevator. "Wait.
What?"

"We traced it to a company in Seattle. It's owned
by Mr. Sterling's brother."

Clay felt as though his heart had stopped beating. Astrid had been right. And this also meant that

they had a serious problem on their hands. For some unknown reason, Johnathon's brother, Andrew, was trying to sabotage the company. "Wow. Thank you. Can we talk about this tomorrow? I have somewhere I needed to be like five minutes ago." Maybe ten.

"Sure thing, Mr. Morgan."

Clay hopped on board and jabbed the button for the garage, nearly sprinting out to his car when he arrived. The elevator and the parking deck were both notorious dead zones, and he had to call Astrid to keep her from leaving her apartment. He didn't get the chance though. Miranda called him first.

"Miranda," he blurted, pulling out onto the street. "I can't talk right now."

"Have you talked to Astrid? She's leaving. For Norway. Right now."

"I know. I'm on my way to her apartment. I'm hoping to stop her." He shot a look over his shoulder and changed lanes to get around a slow driver.

"She's already on her way to the airport."

"What? No." *Dammit.* He was pointed in the wrong direction, and so much of downtown San Diego was one-way streets. "Are you sure?"

"She was just here. She came by to tell me she was giving her shares of Sterling to the baby."

It was so much worse than he thought. That did not sound like the action of a woman who was planning on coming back. "I have to go to the airport."

"Of course you do. That's why I was calling."

Despite the urgency of the moment, he had to

laugh at the absurdity of it, and that his sister was just as invested in this as he was. "You're sure you're okay with Astrid? Did you two have a chance to talk things through?" He impatiently waited for the light to turn green, drumming his thumbs on the steering wheel. "I need to know that right now. Because I have a lot to tell Astrid as soon as I find her."

"I can't believe you would even ask me that. Would you really let my happiness stand in the way of yours?"

What kind of question was that? "Of course I would, Miranda. You are the one person who has always been there for me. I would do anything for you."

"Okay, then. I want you to stop worrying about Delia and me and start worrying about yourself. You can't make Delia happy if you're not happy, and you sure as hell can't make me happy either."

Somewhere in his brain was that same bit of information, but he'd been unable to reach it before. "I hate it when you're right."

"I'm sorry it happens so often."

"Very funny." He was finally headed in the right direction, but he realized he'd forgotten one important detail. "Dammit. I was supposed to pick up Delia from school. Can you do it? I'll come right over to your house when I'm done at the airport."

"If you do it right, you should not be coming to see me after you find Astrid."

"Miranda. Are you seriously trying to talk about

sex right now? Because I'm not discussing that with you."

"Don't be an idiot. That's all I ask. Now go."

"Hold on, Miranda. One more thing. I found out the source of the email you got on Monday. It came from Andrew's company up in Seattle."

"I don't understand."

"I don't either, but we're going to need to sort it out. I think he's trying to sabotage Sterling Enterprises. As to why, I do not know, but I think there's a chance he was behind our problems with the Seaport project."

"So Astrid was right all along? All the more reason you need to get to the airport."

"Yeah, I know. I'm on it." He bid goodbye to Miranda and focused on the road. As he ran through yellow lights and made a few risky maneuvers with his car, all he could think about was that he had no idea where to even start with Astrid. There were fifty different things going through his head, all of which started with a long string of apologies.

As he pulled up to the terminal, there were dozens of cars stacked up to drop off passengers. He'd stupidly whizzed right past the valet, and if he tried to circle back around, he could lose at least fifteen minutes. Maybe more.

He was just going to have to make a sacrifice— his car. He zipped around the thick of the traffic jam, then angled between two cars and squeezed into an impossibly tight spot. Not only was the security guard standing on the curb, he was watching him. *Of course.* Clay hopped out and started to run inside.

"Hey! You can't leave your vehicle," the officer said as he jogged past.

"Tow it if you want," Clay shouted back. "I have to find the love of my life." He kept going, not waiting for a response. Consequences were for later. He'd already suffered plenty from his own bullheadedness. Inside, Clay was confronted by the chaos of hundreds of travelers, dragging suitcases behind them and absentmindedly blocking traffic while they stared up at departure boards. He zigged and zagged around people, quickly scanning the baggage check-in lines. There was no sign of Astrid. Hope was evaporating with every second. If she was here, she was getting closer and closer to getting on her plane. And then it occurred to him—he was doing this all wrong.

He pulled out his cell phone and called her number. It rang. And rang. The buzz of the line was about to drive him nuts, when she finally answered. "Clay? What do you want?"

"Where are you?"

"Why do you want to know?"

"Because I love you and I'm an idiot and we have to talk."

"This is horrible timing, Clay. I'm at the airport. I'm about to get on a flight to Norway."

"I know that. I read your letter. I'm at the airport, too."

"I didn't leave that for you so you'd follow me. I was just trying to explain myself. Are you crazy?"

"Probably. Actually, definitely. Just tell me where you are."

"In line for security, about to turn over my passport."

"Don't move an inch. I'll be there in one minute."

Security had taken forever. Astrid was typically able to take the line for first class, but they had closed it today. Something about a shortage of agents. Astrid wasn't about to complain. She was fine waiting as long as everyone else did, but it had dragged on and on forever. Her fellow passengers were all voicing their displeasure at the delay, grumbling under their breaths and standing on tiptoe to see what the problem was ahead. Astrid kept looking in the opposite direction, wondering if Clay was really there. Would he do something so desperate? It didn't seem like him at all. She was next in line when she heard his voice.

"Astrid!" Clay Morgan, the man who was reserved to a fault, was currently shouting her name in the middle of a crowded airport.

She couldn't help but laugh. She thrust her hand up in the air and waved back, only to see him trying to wind his way through the stanchions, past the other passengers, one by one. He was lucky no one was picking a fight with him.

"Don't move." His gaze connected with hers,

sending a zip of electricity through her. Damn him for being so irresistible. Damn him for being everything she ever wanted.

Astrid turned to the woman in line behind her. "That's that man I fell in love with."

"He's not going with you on the trip?"

"I think he's trying to prevent it."

"And is that a good thing or a bad thing?" she asked.

"Depends on how good he is at groveling." It was Astrid's turn to present her boarding pass and passport, but Clay had just reached her.

"Please don't get on that flight," he blurted. "We have to talk."

The other passengers griped in near unison.

"Ma'am, I either need your boarding pass or you need to step out of line," the agent said. "But I'm warning you that if you step out, you have to go back to the very end."

Astrid let the woman behind her go ahead, then turned to Clay. "Well?"

"I promise I will make it worth it." Breathless, he grabbed her hand, unhooked the black retractable strap from the stanchion, and pulled her back in the direction where she'd started.

Astrid stumbled ahead, lugging her carry-on. "I can't believe you would try to hunt me down at the airport. What has gotten into you?" This was so unlike anything she'd ever seen Clay do, it was hard to wrap her head around. Still, she found it to be quite thrilling that he would be willing to embarrass himself in public like this. It had to mean something.

They came to a stop once they'd reached the wide concourse between check-in and baggage claim.

Clay turned to her. "I love you, Astrid. I've been falling in love with you since the car ride to Los Angeles, if I'm perfectly honest." He looked up at the ceiling and shook his head. It was like he was processing everything in real time. She'd always loved watching him think. "Or maybe it was the night of the cocktail party at Grant's house. Either way, I'm over the moon for you and I'm begging you to stay. You are everything I have ever wanted and I will be lost without you. Please don't move back to Norway. I'm begging you."

"I told you I wasn't necessarily moving. This trip was to clear my head."

"I think I know another way to clear your head." Before she knew what was happening, Clay pulled her into his arms, pressing his long form against hers and laying the deepest, most passionate kiss on her that she'd ever been on the receiving end of. He cradled the back of her head with his hand, all while she virtually melted into him. When he broke the kiss, he didn't let her go far, holding on to her tight. Their mouths were mere inches apart, his breath warm on her lips. "Well?"

"If anything, that's just you trying to confuse me."

He laughed quietly and pressed another kiss to the corner of her mouth. "Did it work? Did I buy myself some time?"

Astrid dropped her shoulders. She had no energy to fight him. She only wanted to give in. But they had things to sort out. "I'm going to miss my flight, so yes. You bought yourself some time. The question is what you intend to do with it."

"I'll do whatever you want. I'm serious. I love you, Astrid." He tenderly combed his fingers through her hair. "I should have told you long ago. I was scared. I can admit that now. And when your secret came out, it felt like confirmation of everything I'd feared. It felt like it was all happening again."

"And now? How do you feel now?"

"Like I need to learn to look past what's right in front of my face and try to see what's truly ahead. Try to see the future, not spend all of my time reliving the past."

Astrid swallowed hard, choking back the emotion of the moment. She not only loved hearing him say these things to her, she admired the way he'd put it all together for himself. He'd fought hard to tear off the blinders, rather than clinging to the idea of keeping them on. "I love you so much. I don't really know how to put it into words." She took his hand and pressed it to her chest. "But I hope that you can feel my heart beating. That's all for you. It's all possible because of you. I won't go anywhere if that's what you want."

"That's what I want. Always."

She hadn't prepared herself for that last word, especially on a day like today, when she'd been sure she was leaving and that would be the end of it. To make things even more surreal, it was then that Clay, the proudest man she knew, dropped to his knee, right there in the middle of the airport. He took her hand and peered up at her with his deep and soulful eyes. "I don't have a ring to offer you right now, Astrid, but I can offer you myself. My undivided attention. My heart and everything that goes along with that, good or bad."

"Careful, Clay. You're practically reciting wedding vows." She leaned down and pressed her hand to the cheek of the man who had once held so much mystery. "Your sister told me the quickest way to freak you out is to mention marriage."

He shook his head. "Nope. The only thing that will put me into a panic is the thought of you leaving."

She smiled so wide her cheeks hurt. "Then let's get out of here." He straightened and took her hand, but she stopped before they got to the glass doors. "Oh, shoot. My bags. I've already checked them. They're probably already on the plane."

"Actually, that works out pretty well because I'm pretty sure my car has been towed."

"What?"

He shrugged. "I was in a hurry."

They did stop by the airline baggage desk to let them know of the change in plans. Luckily, her suitcases had not yet been loaded, and they could retrieve them and deliver them for a fee. Clay handed over his credit card. "It's my fault. I'll pay for it."

The clerk nodded and handed over a form for Astrid to fill out. "If you could provide your delivery address, that would be great."

Clay took that and plucked a pen from the holder on the desk, writing down his home address.

"This is moving very fast," Astrid joked.

He lowered his head with no regard for the people around them. Astrid was fine with that. Right now, he was her whole world. He nudged her nose with his before delivering a tender, leg-melting kiss. "I'm not stupid, Astrid. I'm not letting you out of my sight."

* * * * *

*Don't miss the next story in
Karen Booth's miniseries,
The Sterling Wives:*

All He Wants for Christmas

Available from Harlequin Desire!

#2767 CLAIMING THE RANCHER'S HEIR
Gold Valley Vineyards • by Maisey Yates
It's Christmas and rancher Creed Cooper must work with his rival, Wren Maxfield—so tempers flare! But animosity becomes passion and, now, Wren is pregnant. Creed wants a marriage in name only. But as desire takes over, this may be a vow neither can keep...

#2768 IN BED WITH HIS RIVAL
Texas Cattleman's Club: Rags to Riches
by Katherine Garbera
With a bitter legal battle between their families, lawyer Brian Cooper knows he should stay away from Piper Holloway. For Piper, having a fling with a younger man is fun...until stunning truths are revealed. Now can she ever trust him with her heart?

#2769 SLOW BURN
Dynasties: Seven Sins • by Janice Maynard
Jake Lowell has been a globe-trotting playboy for years, ignoring all his family obligations. Until he learns his one hot night with hardworking Nikki Reardon resulted in a child. Will his history threaten a future with the woman who got away?

#2770 VOWS IN NAME ONLY
Billionaires of Boston • by Naima Simone
When CEO Cain Farrell is blackmailed into marrying his enemy's daughter, he vows it will be a marriage on paper only. But one sizzling kiss with Devon Cole changes everything. Can he look past her father's sins to build a real future together?

#2771 THE SINNER'S SECRET
Bad Billionaires • by Kira Sinclair
Wrongly convicted executive Gray Lockwood will stop at nothing to prove his innocence, including working with the woman who put him behind bars, accountant Blakely Whittaker. But now this billionaire realizes he doesn't just want justice, he wants her...

#2772 ALL HE WANTS FOR CHRISTMAS
The Sterling Wives • by Karen Booth
Andrew Sterling wants one thing: to destroy his dead brother's company. But when his brother's widow, Miranda, invites Andrew over for the holidays, attraction ignites. He'll have to choose between the woman in his bed and the resentment that has guided him until now...

---

*It's Christmas and rancher Creed Cooper must work
with his rival, Wren Maxfield—and tempers flare! But
animosity becomes passion and, now, Wren is pregnant.
Creed wants a marriage in name only. But as desire
takes over, this may be a vow neither can keep...*

Read on for a sneak peek at
Claiming the Rancher's Heir
by New York Times *bestselling author Maisey Yates!*

"Come here," he said, his voice suddenly hard. "I want to show
you something."

There was a big white tent that was still closed, reserved for
an evening hors d'oeuvre session for people who had bought
premium tickets, and he compelled her inside. It was already set
up with tables and tablecloths, everything elegant and dainty,
and exceedingly Maxfield. Though there were bottles of Cowboy
Wines on each table, along with bottles of Maxfield select.

But they were not apparently here to look at the wine, or indeed
anything else that was set up. Which she discovered when he
cupped her chin with firm fingers and looked directly into her eyes.

"I've done nothing but think about you for two weeks. I want
you. Not just something hot and quick against a wall. I need you
in a bed, Wren. We need some time to explore this. To explore
each other."

She blinked. She had not expected that.

He'd been avoiding her and she'd been so sure it was because
he didn't want this.

But he was here in a suit.

And he had a look of intent gleaming in those green eyes.

She realized then she'd gotten it all wrong.

"I…I agree."

She also hadn't expected to agree.

"I want you now," she whispered, and before she could stop herself, she was up on her tiptoes and kissing that infuriating mouth.

She wanted to sigh with relief. She had been so angry at him. So angry at the way he had ignored this. Because how dare he? He had never ignored the anger between them. No. He had taken every opportunity to goad and prod her in anger. So why, why had he ignored this?

But he hadn't.

They were devouring each other, and neither of them cared that there were people outside. His large hands palmed her ass, pulling her up against his body so she could feel just how hard he was for her. She arched against him, gasping when the center of her need came into contact with his rampant masculinity.

She didn't understand the feelings she had for this man. Where everything about him that she found so disturbing was also the very thing that drove her into his arms.

Too big. Too rough. Crass. Untamable. He was everything she detested, everything she desired.

All that, and he was distracting her from an event that she had planned. Which was a cardinal sin in her book. And she didn't even care.

He set her away from him suddenly, breaking their kiss. "Not now," he said, his voice rough. "Tonight. All night. You. In my bed."

Don't miss what happens next in…
Claiming the Rancher's Heir
by New York Times *bestselling author Maisey Yates!*

Available November 2020 wherever
Harlequin Desire books and ebooks are sold.

Harlequin.com

Love Harlequin romance?

DISCOVER.

Be the first to find out about promotions, news and exclusive content!

 Facebook.com/HarlequinBooks

Twitter.com/HarlequinBooks

 Instagram.com/HarlequinBooks

Pinterest.com/HarlequinBooks

ReaderService.com

EXPLORE.

Sign up for the Harlequin e-newsletter and download a free book from any series at **TryHarlequin.com**

CONNECT.

Join our Harlequin community to share your thoughts and connect with other romance readers!
Facebook.com/groups/HarlequinConnection

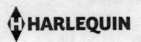